# artemis dreamt

# artemis dream

crystal beran

RainTown Press

This book is a work of fiction. All names, characters, places, and incidents are either the product of the author's imagination or are used fictitiously. Any resemblance to actual events, business establishments, locales, or persons, living or dead, is entirely coincidental.



Published by RainTown Press, Portland, Oregon's premier independent press dedicated to publishing classic and original literature for middle grade and young adult readers.

On a more serious note: At RainTown Press, our favorite kind of journey is one of self-discovery—better yet, one that can be taken by motorcycle. In theory, you could take a trip up the I-5 corridor and stop at every point you read about in this book (which you should do anyway, it's beautiful country), *or*, you could bust out on a journey of your own, but still take this book with you because it's going to change your world... *or at least how you view it.*

For information regarding permissions, please write:

RainTown Press

1111 E. Burnside St. #309 • Portland, OR 97214

You can also visit us *via the web at* www.raintownpress.com, facebook.com/raintownpress or @raintownpress on twitter

ISBN [hardcover] 978-1-939089-04-5

ISBN [epub: nook etc.] 978-1-939089-05-2

ISBN [mobi: kindle]: 978-1-939089-06-9

CIP data available

Typeset in:

Adobe Caslon Pro, Century Gothic, and Contempo Jungle Minuet

Printed by Bang Printing in the United States of America

Printed on FSC-certified paper (it's a green thing.)

FOR RYAN

# PART ONE

# DAY ONE

It rained.

All afternoon the clouds swelled until they were so heavy they bobbed low in the sky, so low you could stand on a ladder and pop them with pins. But not one drop of rain fell until the dirt brown Dodge pulled out of our driveway. As it drove away from us, its oversized antenna snagged on a cloud and ripped a hole from here to Reno. Then the water dumped out of the sky in buckets and swimming pools and oceans. If it kept up like this, I was going to need a boat.

I hesitated for a moment in the failing light of evening. No one told me to come inside or to put on a jacket, so I stood on the porch wearing only a tank top, shorts, and checkered rubber boots. Every few seconds, a raindrop squeezed through the leak in the roof and hit me in the arm, leaving behind goose bumps the size of mosquito bites.

The sheet of rain came tumbling down so thick I couldn't see Mr. Lennitz's cherry red Corvette across the street. Still,

I knew it was there, peeking out from under its sheet. It really is such a restful car. It sleeps and sleeps all bundled up in its blanket until Mr. Lennitz wakes it on Sunday afternoons for a drive around the block and a bath. When he's done, he tucks it back in and kisses it good night for another week.

My yard is about as diametrically opposite as you can get. Cars come here to die. They litter the yard with their mechanical guts hanging out—rivers of entrails spilling down into the storm drains. I am not Artemis in this kingdom of rust. I have become Partemis: Queen of the Junkers.

We have four broken cars and one that still runs. My father brought them home one at a time, like stray dogs, and spent his Saturdays fixing them up. He wasn't any good at it, but he did bring the Mustang back to life—just once.

It was summer, and I was reading about a girl with a crumbling down house on Mango Street when he called me outside.

"Get in the driver's seat."

I looked back through the open door to where my brother, Prince, lay sleeping on the carpet. "I'm supposed to be watching the baby."

"It'll only take a minute."

He tossed the keys to me, but I missed and had to dig them out of the gravel. We hadn't paved the driveway yet.

"Get in," he said again, holding the door open for me.

I climbed inside, stuffed the key into the ignition, and woke the lion.

"That's it, Art. Now hit the gas."

"I can't drive." He was standing in front of the car; I was going to run him over.

"It's in neutral. You're not going anywhere, kiddo. Hit the gas."

I was so short I had to slump all the way down in the driver's seat to reach the pedals. From down there, all I could see was the steering wheel and the sky.

A few days later, we took her for a spin; but she died in front of the 7-Eleven, and we had to call a tow truck to bring us home.

He doesn't work on them anymore. Now his spare time is consumed by the game, can after can of watery beer, and long, abrupt absences. So the cars sit out in the yard, and the green things slowly creep up and reclaim them piece by piece.

I stepped off the porch and into the rain.

At my feet was a stone caked with dirt. I picked it up. In the downpour, the mud melted away, and, as I turned it over, I saw that it was not a stone at all. It was a chunk of concrete.

It didn't matter. It was heavy and it was hard.

I threw it right at the Mustang propped up on blocks. Through the roar of the rain, the smash was nearly inaudible; but I felt it in my chest, and it was more satisfying than I thought it would be. I approached to survey the damage.

I had popped the left headlight; it bled little bits of glass onto the ground.

I reached for another chunk of concrete. Popped its right eye. Another. Cracked its window. Again. Caved in a piece of the door. Soon, loose chunks became hard to find, so I had to dig them out of the ground. Smash. Smash. Smash. Pop, pop: its taillights.

More. I needed more. The shadow beneath the car concealed a piece of concrete the size of my head. I pried it loose, forcing dirt and gravel up under my fingernails. It was too heavy to throw, so I lifted it as high as I could manage and dropped it on the hood. Again and again I let the boulder fall until the car was as cratered as the moon.

Still armed, I turned to the Viper. I pounded it with the big slab of concrete until my arms finally gave out. Then I collected all the small pieces I'd already thrown and threw them again. Everything was shattered glass and dented metal.

Exhausted, I climbed onto the battered hood of the Viper and paused to catch my breath. I was still clinging to one last chunk of concrete, squeezing it as hard as I could, so hard it hurt.

Grinding my teeth, I pounded the concrete into the center of the Viper's windshield until all the glass was dust.

When I finally let the stone roll out of my hand, I found a single line of blood etched across the middle of my palm. The line was surprisingly straight, as if I'd carved it with a scalpel. Rain and blood mixed into a pool in my opened hand—like colored dye swirling into cups of vinegar at Easter. I liked the way it looked. I picked the concrete back up, found the sharp edge, and cut a straight line on the inside of my forearm.

As the light of day succumbed to the night, I sat on the broken shell of the Viper and watched a small row of notches creep closer and closer to my elbow.

When I licked the rain from my lips, I tasted salt.

# NIGHT ONE

Prince turned six today. They forgot again. I knew they would. Birthdays aren't so much a thing for us, but they could have at least gotten him a card or told him to have a good day at school. I stopped at the grocery store on my way home and picked out a small square of carrot cake, paying extra to have them write his name in frosting. At home, I slid the three-by-three plastic box into the fridge. I hadn't worked up the courage to give it to him yet; I didn't want to disturb him.

He'd been sitting scrunched up on the second shelf of the hall closet since five, talking softly to his rabbit, Walker, who munched on a carrot and grunted in agreement every now and then. It felt like trespassing, coming between Prince and Walker, like intruding on a secret whispered more out of politeness than confidentiality because I wouldn't have understood anyway.

The Game Show Network was blaring at full volume. I tiptoed down the hall and into the kitchen. It was almost nine. Our mother was still on the couch drinking vodka as if nothing had happened. I peeked under one of the Band-Aids on my arm. I had not imagined it.

The carrot cake was even smaller than I remembered it. But it was just for Prince. He wouldn't have to share it with anyone. I pulled the box out and cupped it in my hands as if it were a baby bird.

"Prince?" I cooed, creeping up to him. In my bare feet, my footsteps were soft. But my heart thundered against my ribs. I was afraid he'd shut the door again, hide himself in the darkness of his warren where only he and Walker were allowed.

He didn't answer, but he stopped jabbering to his rabbit.

"Hey, Prince," I tried again, smiling to feign a courage I did not feel. "I have something for you."

Walker eyed me suspiciously.

"It's a cake. It's your birthday. Happy birthday."

Prince tilted his face toward me but didn't raise his eyes to mine. The blood on his forehead had dulled to the color of rust so it was hard to tell which of the brown streaks were dirt from the garden and which were worse. A bruise was forming. What would he tell his teacher? I forgot all about the cake in my hands.

"You don't have to take a bath tonight, but we need to get your face cleaned up. You can't go to school with blood on you. They'll take you away."

☽ ☽ ☽

When I got back from school this afternoon, our father was on the phone with his girlfriend and our mother was plunging her hand into a jar of olives, enjoying her 3:30 martini straight from the bottle. Our father paced back and forth behind her, bellowing into his cell phone.

"No, you stupid bitch, of course I can't do that. What do you think I am?... Well, maybe I would if you weren't such... You think I don't know what you did?... No, don't say that. You know I don't mean it. You know how I get, baby. It's not my fault... Well, why don't you tell him that... I hate *you*... Shut up. Just shut up for a minute... Baby... I'll be there in a half hour... Baby, come on. You don't mean that... You know I don't... Her? She's a fucking drunk. She doesn't know anything... Of course I don't love her... No, baby, it's only you I love... Them? I don't give a fuck about them... You know I can't do that... We've talked about this... Think of the child support ..."

He would have gone on another half an hour like he usually does, but this time my mother got up, snatched the phone away from him, flicked on the garbage disposal, and tossed the phone down the drain.

The disposal choked and gasped for water as it gagged on jagged pieces of silver plastic.

I wanted to run away, to escape into the safety of my room, but my feet wouldn't budge. There was nothing to do but watch.

My father grabbed hold of my mother's arms and, for a moment, I thought he was going to throw her in after it. Instead, he pulled her into the living room and tipped her over the backside of the couch. She rolled to the floor, taking the pillows with her, and then she went after him again—screaming and throwing punches but too drunk to land a solid blow. He didn't hit her back; he just swatted her arms away each time she swung for him.

From out of nowhere, Prince slipped between them. If he spoke, I couldn't hear it. With one hand our father picked up my baby brother and launched him into the other room. He skidded across the wood floor and came to a stop a few feet from me.

I just stood there. I didn't help him up. I couldn't move.

Casually, our father picked his coat up off the back of his armchair like he was just headed out for the evening. He switched the garbage disposal off.

The absence of sound roared louder than the cacophony from a moment ago, and, in that eerie silence, my father walked out the back door, caught the screen so it wouldn't slam, and drove away.

I listened to the car rumble down the street, turn left at the stop sign, and merge quietly onto the highway a half mile away.

That's when Prince, the quietest little boy I've ever met, screamed.

"Shut up," our mother ordered him, and the sound became the choking of a small animal. "Miss," she said, her eyes on the vodka bottle, "clean up your brother. I gotta lie down."

I didn't listen. I ran out into the rain.

◡ ◡ ◡

"PRINCE?" I TRIED AGAIN, FEELING smaller than a speck of dust. "Prince, come on, we've got to wash off your face."

He held his hand out to me. "Wipe," he ordered.

"Okay, I'll get you a wipe."

But when I returned, he'd shut the door on me, and I dared not open it. I left the cake out for him, but it was still there, untouched, in the morning.

# DAY TWO

The laundry had been piling up for weeks. This morning I had to dig all the way to the bottom of Prince's clothes hamper to find something that wasn't too filthy for him to wear to school. His red and white striped shirt was red and white and brown; his blue jeans had green knees. His clothes were covered in dirt from all the time he spent breathing life into the small square of earth he'd transformed into his garden. If there were flowers to pick or seeds to plant, Prince was up to his ears in them.

The Superman shirt wasn't too bad; the black background hid the soil stains at least. It didn't really matter, though. The dust of ancient civilizations followed Prince around no matter what you did to scrub him or his clothes clean.

I rubbed the blood off his face as best I could, got him dressed, and then sent him skipping off down the sidewalk toward school. That's when I realized I had a history project due. A history project I had already received one extension on. A history project I had yet to start. Miss Gonzales would want to talk to me after class in a soft, worried voice about my future and the value of the education I was wasting. She was going to try to guilt me into taking a second extension. Ugh. I wish teachers would just give zeroes like they used to.

Of course, I could avoid such an intrusion of my personal space by avoiding school altogether. I shoveled the laundry together in a big pile, stuffed it in the sidecar of my motorcycle, and headed downtown.

There was only one parking space left, closer to the front of the liquor store than the Laundromat, and directly next to a black and white cruiser. I pulled in carefully, forcing my hands to remain steady as I unclasped my helmet and hung it off the handlebars askance, like it was no big thing.

I didn't dare raise my eyes; I just kept looking down: down at the kickstand, down at the sidecar, down at the blood stain on Prince's white and blue tee ball shirt. Or maybe that was just a smudge of soil. Or maybe he took a spill careening around third on his way home.

A pair of big, black boots swaggered up to me.

"You ride," Boots told me, as if sharing some secret.

I refused to look up; kept my hands busy in our dirty laundry, searching for something that wasn't there. I found something I didn't mean to, one of Tommy's undershirts. How long had it been since he last came over? I balled it up as tight as I could.

"Aren't you a little young to ride a motorcycle?"

"Not according to my license."

My eyes flicked up to his face as he took two steps closer. He hid behind the steam rising off his coffee though he wore no sunglasses, not in the gray light of morning. His eyes were empty mirrors.

I have a sneaking suspicion that the police are robots.

"I'd like to see that license," he snarled as he stepped even closer to me.

Nobody had taught him about personal space. Nobody had taught him about coffee breath. I feigned pleasantness; if you try to run or fight, they'll know you're lying. "Of course, officer. Is there anything wrong?"

I slipped the license out of my wallet, hiding my school ID from his line of vision. My graduation year was printed across the top, and the numbers on the two cards didn't exactly match up.

"How old are you?" he asked, angling the license to look for holograms.

"Sixteen."

"When were you born?"

I rattled off the numbers printed on the license like I owned them.

"You go to school?"

"No. I couldn't handle classes and a full-time job so I dropped out. But I passed the proficiency exam and I'm looking into community college."

"You live with your parents?"

Did I? "My uncle."

He stopped asking me questions but continued to frown at the picture on the card and then at me. "You just don't look a day older than fourteen."

"I get that a lot. I'll be laughing when I'm thirty, won't I?" But he was right. I was fourteen.

A faint smile swept across his lips. It made him look like a lizard. "You sure will." He returned my license, leaning over the side of my bike in that way cops do because they all think they're your father. "You enroll in community college, you hear. Do well in your classes, get your degree, and make something of yourself."

"Will do," I told him, and waved goodbye until I no longer had the desire to spit at his car. It took a while. He'd already pulled out onto the street before I put my hand down.

Danger averted. I rolled the ball of clothes into the center of a row of empty washers. Except for Tommy's shirt. I left that out in the street. An old woman sat on the bench, watching her clothes tumble around in the dryer. She didn't ask me why I wasn't in school or where my mother was as I dropped quarter after quarter through the slots. I smiled at her, but she wasn't looking. By the time I'd started up all six washers she was gone.

Alone, I sat and watched the suds form through the windows. Sometimes there were pieces of the newspaper strewn about, but today there were only discarded Christian magazines to choose from. I tried reading one backwards to look for hidden messages. There didn't seem to be any, so I packed up the dryers and watched those too.

When everything came out hot and dry, I dumped the clothes into a big pile and burrowed into the center to feel their warmth, to let it seep all the way into my heart, but the heat never lasted long enough.

# NIGHT TWO

“Hello?”

I paused at the threshold of the round, unfamiliar room. It took a moment for my eyes to adjust; the single florescent light did little to banish the darkness and nothing to banish the cold. There were no corners, the walls just sort of curved in on each other, almost as if I was inside an egg. I took a sharp breath in, squeezed my mother’s hand, and forced myself to take a few steps forward. Behind us, the airlock slid shut and locked from the other side.

“Hello?” I said again, looking for the welcoming party that wasn’t there. *Hadn’t they sent for us?* “Is anyone here?”

I moved toward the center of the empty space, each step kicking up a painful, metallic clang that reverberated through the station. I felt like I was ringing the dinner bell. Come and get it. On either side of the airlock, four perfectly round portholes peered in on the blackness, like the rows of shiny, unblinking eyes on a spider. We could see nothing that swam around in the deep but the bottom-dwelling beasts could peep in on us as they pleased.

My mother chewed on the end of her thumb.

"Hello. Is there anyone there?" Tears welled up in the corners of my eyes, but I refused to let them fall, swallowing them instead. I squeezed my eyes shut and counted. *One, two, three.* We were alone but safe inside a well stocked deep-sea station. *Four, five.* Another dive team was sure to come along. *Six.* We might even be able to repair the broken communications equipment. *Seven.* My mother is pretty handy. *Eight—*

A man's voice called out to me from somewhere behind a closed door. "Hello. Sorry, just a minute." His footsteps clanged through the corridor. "You're here."

I let out the breath I didn't realize I was holding and took in another one. "What happened?"

"Not the warm welcome you were expecting? Yeah. So sorry about that. I'm afraid it's just me." He shuffled his coffee to his left hand and grasped my right in his, pulling me closer—too close. The coffee had grown stale. I could smell it on his breath.

"Just you? Where are the other scientists?"

His eyes were the same black mirrors that hung along the walls. "I'm very sorry. There's been an accident."

"An accident?"

"It's just me."

I tried to pull my hand out of his, but his grip was stone. "What? What happened?"

He looked away, to where my mother stood with her hands cupped on the glass, trying to make a window on the window. "There'll be time for that in the morning. You need to rest." He turned back to me, smiling, just not with his eyes. "Come. I'll show you to your rooms."

I tried to swallow, but my throat was so dry I gagged on the back of my own tongue.

He led us through a narrow corridor and opened the door to a small bedroom with a large, black window. "Prince can sleep here," he said.

Prince. That's right. He'd come with us. I'd forgotten. How had I forgotten?

"And your mother, she'll sleep here. Your room is the big one." He led me inside and stood in front of the window with his hands behind his back as if he were admiring the view. "We'll get this sorted out. Don't you worry."

"What's going to happen now?"

He didn't seem to hear me. "There she is," he said, pointing into the dark. "There, do you see her?"

There was nothing to see. "No."

"Wait for it. Wait. There." He tapped the glass, the way they always tell you not to at the zoo. "No? Oh well. Soon enough."

His hand clamped down on my shoulder, a friendly gesture that he hadn't practiced well. I flinched. His fingertips were like ice after touching the glass.

"We'll talk in the morning. The kitchen's at the end of the hall if you need anything."

"It's called a galley," I said, but I was alone.

Sleep evaded me. It wasn't supposed to be like this. We'd caught a break, my mother and I. We were finally going to be able to work together, side by side, to make a difference in the world, to do something worth remembering. We wouldn't get a chance like this again.

That night, I lay in bed for what seemed like hours and looked out the window pointlessly. All I could see was my own dim reflection. Maybe a snack would help me take my mind off things.

The hall was longer than I remembered. Darker, too. About halfway to the galley, my shoes started sticking to the floor. There wasn't enough light to see why, but, then, I didn't really want to know anyway.

In the galley, the light was already on. I could see it through the crack running all the way around the edge of the door. Somebody else was up.

"There's been no accident," I whispered to myself.

I reached the door, slowly turned the handle and, pressing my cheek against the cold metal, opened it just enough to see inside.

At first, all I could see was shoes. His: black, shiny, cold—as if the darkness from out there followed him wherever he went and pooled around his feet.

The second set of shoes were the size of my hands, the Spiderman emblem just discernible under a layer of soil.

With one hand, the empty-eyed man lifted my brother up off the ground. Prince's chubby legs kicked beneath him, as if he were trying to run to me. He struggled there for a moment and then went limp.

My mind drifted. I thought of a nature show I saw once about wolves. It was winter and some of them were so starved that their fur was falling out in patches. If they didn't catch something soon, they were all going to die. Finally, just when it looked like they weren't going to make it, they caught a young elk. They pinned it down in the snow and snapped and snarled at each other, and some began to tear chunks of flesh from the elk's hind legs. He just sat there and watched. He didn't try to escape; he didn't fight back at all. They ate him alive and he just watched.

That's how Prince looked hanging there, watching the man pick up a long, thin knife. He didn't plead or cry or anything. He just watched.

The man slid the knife back and forth across his pant leg. Scrape. Scrape. Scrape. Scrape. He would not be rushed.

He held my brother a little farther away, tracing the knife first up, then down Prince's back. When he let him drop, Prince's spine dangled neatly on the point of the knife. There wasn't even any blood.

I'd been invisible up to that point, just an observer. Not anymore. Black eyes locked with mine. This was my nightmare now.

It took him only three enormous steps to reach the door.

I ran.

But I knew that there was nowhere to go. Every door along the hall was locked. I was still tugging on the one that led to my mother's room when he caught me.

His fingers wrapped around my arm like snakes.

"No, no, no, no." I scratched at the walls, trying to dig a hole into the bottom of the ocean.

"It's a good thing you came when you did. I'd run out."

"Mom! Mom! Come out! I need you. Mom!" My voice broke off, and the tears flowed like the ocean I couldn't reach.

My eyes were squeezed shut, but I could see him anyway, raising the knife and plunging it in between my ribs, all the way to my heart where the suddenness of the pain stopped everything.

☽ ☽ ☽

THE SCREEN DOOR SMACKED AGAINST the house like the crack of a gunshot. I wasn't stuck at the bottom of the ocean but I may as well have been, swimming in sweat as I was. The panic wasn't easing off fast enough but already the gruesome images were beginning to fade.

*My mother the scientist. Ha.*

It was just past midnight. My mother the drunk had failed to catch the screen door on her way out.

# DAY THREE

"Did you get the note I left you?"

It was Jason Messenger. I frowned at him through the unopened screen.

"I left you a note."

My gaze sunk to the floor. He had left a note along with a picture he took of me riding home from the Laundromat. I had hidden it away in the drawer with the others.

He put his hand gently against the screen where my shoulder was two feet farther away.

"Yeah, I got your note."

"Are you busy? Do you want to hang out?"

"No."

"No what? No, you're not busy or—"

"No both."

There's a button on the handle of the screen door. I traced my thumb around its perimeter, keeping my eyes away from Jason's. He had dog eyes, the kind that make you want to feed him and take him along in the car even if you're just going to the store. The button fit perfectly under my thumb. I covered it and uncovered it and pressed it just as hard as I could without opening the door.

Jason watched me watch my thumb not push the button for a long time before he finally turned and walked away. He made me so tired, and every time he left it was as if he'd taken an ice cream scoop sized part of me and turned it out onto the ground. It didn't use to be that way. We used to play bike tag and rock drop and snail race up and down the street until his mom called him in for dinner. I stood there, watching the space he left behind for the better part of an hour, wondering why he had to try so damn hard. It wasn't his fault. Time had simply eaten away at our childhoods until we were left with all of the worry of adulthood and none of the freedom. After awhile, his mother's blue van drove past my doorway, and I crept out to the mailbox.

Amidst the junk, advertisements, and third-and-final notices there was a nondescript envelope addressed to me. It had been sent from Delaware. I don't know anyone in Delaware but a month ago I received a letter in the mail. "You've already been approved for a credit line of up to $5,000!"

I drifted back into the house, dumping all the mail but mine in the recycling bin, and opened my letter to find my very first credit card. I'd lied about my age and my annual household income and forged my mother's signature as a cosigner, and the company had sent me a $1,500 plastic allowance. I didn't think it would be so easy.

I slipped the card into my tiger-striped vinyl wallet with my fake ID, two dollars cash, and the ticket stubs from all the movies I had seen this year.

My own credit card. It looked good in there.

# NIGHT THREE

THE PARTY STARTED AT TEN. I wanted to get there early but I was having the worst time figuring out my shoes. They had me surrounded, dozens of pairs spiraling out around the room, none of them the ones I wanted. I kept putting them on and taking them off again. This pair looked all right, but one of the heels broke as soon as I stood up. These would have been perfect if they were black instead of hot pink. These made my feet look like witch's feet. They might have worked if I could have ridden a broomstick to the party. When did I get all these useless shoes? At last I settled on a brown pair of clunky heels—ones I hadn't worn before. I didn't even know I had them. I must have stood in front of the mirror for ten minutes frowning at my feet before I finally decided that they'd have to do. Tommy was waiting.

In the living room, my mother was passed out on the couch. A herd of elephants could have marched through the house without rousing her, but I opened the front door quietly anyway.

"Where are you going?" It was Prince. I must have woken him up.

"Go back to bed."

"But where are you going, Artemis?"

I slipped out the front door and into Tommy Nealer's car without answering. It was already midnight.

Tommy drove fast. We spoke of nothing as we zoomed onto the highway, splashing hip-hop out of the open windows. There was simply too much to say.

When we arrived at Dylan's house just a few miles down the road, Tommy turned to me and smiled.

"How do we do this?" I asked, stepping out of the car and straightening myself out.

"What do you mean?"

"Do we go in together? Does one of us go in first? How should we arrive?"

He laughed with just his breath the way he does. "I think you know the answer to that."

"But I don't."

But he didn't hear me. He was already climbing the front steps.

I steadied myself and went in after him.

The place was a madhouse. The whole school must have showed up. Not just the whole school… some kids from Turner, some young college kids home for spring break, and a girl who I knew for a fact was only in eighth grade. Tommy had disappeared into the mob and was nowhere to be seen.

I fished a beer out of the cooler and cracked it open. I don't like beer, but it does take the edge off.

I shouldn't have come. I didn't feel like talking to anybody. I didn't know anybody here.

"You made it."

"Hi, Jason." I swear that boy must have placed a tracking device on me or something.

"You drunk?"

"Nope. Just got here. First beer." I tried to offer him a civil cheers, but he didn't have a drink. Figures.

He smiled at me and then didn't stop smiling the way you do when you don't have anything to say.

"I was thinking—" he began, but I cut him off.

"Is that my mother?"

"What? Your mother?"

Disheveled hair. Animal-print mini skirt. Dark eye shadow and dark lipstick. Bottle of vodka. Yeah, that was definitely my mother. She had her arms around some man. I couldn't see his face.

"What's she doing here?" Jason asked, keeping his back to her. "Are you busted?"

I bit my lip. "I think she's here to party."

As if she heard me, my mother turned to where I stood and we locked eyes. She sloshed over.

"You made it," she said, though her words were slurred.

"Hi, Mom."

"You drunk?"

"Nope. Just got here. First beer."

"Well, get going. You don't have all night."

She stumbled upstairs, the mysterious man a step behind.

"What was that about?" It was Tommy. Ridiculously good-looking Tommy.

I struggled over the thought of telling another sentient human being what had just transpired. Shrugging, I admitted, "My mother likes to party."

He nodded. "She was invited. We all were."

"Well, I don't want her here."

"What do you want?" He turned, giving me all his attention.

The air was so thick I couldn't fit much of it in my lungs at once. "I want you back," I answered at last.

He pulled me close and slipped his soft lips into mine like the gears of a clock. My heart beat out the seconds. He smelled just like a movie star.

Dizzy, I opened my eyes. Tommy's scent still wafted around me, his hand still clung to my waist. I tried to breathe but only sucked more lovely, lovely pheromones into my system.

On the other side of the room, Jason leaned up against a wall, watching us. He smiled kindly and strolled up easily, almost as if he were floating. When he got closer, he gazed deep into my eyes and reached up a hand to brush a stray strand of hair from my face. He didn't say a word, just smiled and then left us.

Tommy pulled me toward the front door. "Come on. We need to leave now."

"Why? We just got here."

He lifted a hand to my mouth. "You can't stay," he insisted, though gently, like he was breaking some terrible news to me that I wouldn't be able to accept.

"I don't understand."

"Jason. Do you love him?"

"What? No! I love you. I still love you."

"What do you want?"

"What do you mean?"

"You don't know." It wasn't a question, just a simple statement of fact because he could see it was true and I could not. "Until you know what you want, you can't stay here."

I couldn't wrap my head around this. "Can't stay where? At Dylan's house? I—"

We were already back in Tommy's car. I sunk down low in the bucket seat, feeling not unlike Prince when we strapped him in to take him to the doctor. As we pulled away from the party, the front wall of Dylan's house melted away, and I could see everything inside. There was my mother, kissing some stranger, oblivious to the world around her. Megan, barely dressed, dancing close with the other cheerleaders egging on the boys with her androgynous sexuality. Hayley, reading quietly in bed, eyeing the phone expectantly. Tommy, yelling crudely at his friends, jumping on the furniture like a monkey, making me hate him. But wait, wasn't Tommy driving the car?

Jason. The only one looking back at me. Standing at the wall that only he and I could see through. Watching me drive away in Tommy Nealer's car.

Tommy sighed softly. He wanted me to understand. "You just can't stay."

# DAY·FOUR

PRINCE RESTED HIS CHIN ON the counter and kept his eyes locked on the toaster.

"I want it cut in pieces. On the lines. And with butter and syrup in every hole."

"I can't cut it on the lines. You're already late for school," I told him, my voice low. "And besides, you're big enough to cut it yourself."

"No. I want you to cut it in pieces. On the lines. And—"

"Prince, that's an unreasonable request. I'm not doing it."

His eyes didn't drift from the machine that could, at any moment, launch a warm, crispy waffle up into the air. "And butter and syrup in every hole."

I rested my palms on the counter, one on either side of him.

"That's how I like them," he reminded me, and the waffle popped out of the toaster. "Cut it on the lines."

I hadn't slept well and I was too tired to argue about waffles, so I took out a knife and fed Prince twenty-four waffle squares, each with butter and syrup in the center.

He frowned when I handed him his plate, but took it anyway, and carried it carefully over to the coffee table so that he could eat with the unconscious body of our mother. She'd gone out again last night, returning just as the sun climbed up from behind Nevada. He didn't wake her, though he hummed to himself while he chewed his breakfast.

When he was done, I helped him into his backpack and sent him off to kindergarten. Once he'd rounded the corner, I headed to my school in the other direction.

Halfway there, I passed one of last night's left-over revelers. He was peeing in a bush, blocking the sidewalk. I could have just crossed the street but I was tired and I wasn't about to let some stinky, hung-over, sidewalk pee-er stand in my way.

"Hey! I'm using this sidewalk for its intended purpose, and you need to shove off and find somewhere less wildly inappropriate to do that."

"A minute," he slurred back.

"Gross."

His zipper snagged halfway up and he swore as he tried to free it. "Piece of shit."

"That about covers it." I stood there, waiting for this mess of a human being to pull himself together so I could continue my walk to school.

He got it, at last, but, just as I went to skid by him, he reached out a greasy hand toward my shoulder. I didn't back up in time. The smell of cigarettes and alcohol and urine and misery made me nauseous.

"You have spunk," he said, leaning even closer into me. "Don't let them take that away from you."

I could still smell him on my clothes all the way to school, like a bad dream chasing me into real life.

☼ ☼ ☼

I FELL ASLEEP IN THE middle of history, and, instead of writing me up or sending me to the principal's office, Miss

Gonzales just let me sleep right there on my desk. After the bell rang and all the other students had left, she woke me by pressing one soft, carefully manicured hand to my shoulder.

"Artemis? Hey," she said, in her best imitation of a Disney princess. "Is everything alright?"

Startled, I lifted my head to find that everyone else was gone. I hate being alone with her. I wish she'd just let it go.

"Everything's fine," I mumbled, sliding my chair back.

She sat down on top of the desk next to mine, blocking any hope of a quick exit. "I'm really concerned about you. Your grades are slipping in all your classes and you've missed a lot of school lately. I gave you two extensions on your report. Did you get it done? No." She paused, her teeth locked around the corner of her lower lip, a carefully selected expression of concern. "Is everything okay at home?"

How could I answer that question?

I paused too long. She read my hesitation as confirmation.

"Is there something I should know?"

I shook my head and tried to shrug like a teenager. "No."

"What happened to you, Artemis? You started out the school year so well."

I shrugged.

"What were you doing all week that you couldn't get your report done?"

The laundry, grocery shopping, preparing meals for me and Prince and our mother, fixing the garbage disposal, smashing cars, dreaming that I was anywhere but where I was. "Nothing."

"You can't let things get away from you like this. Your education is too important. I hate to see you dig yourself these holes, Artemis. You could be an A student, you know? You're very bright. Here's what I'm going to do. I'm giving you until Monday with no late penalty. How's that sound?" Sometimes I think she cares so much about caring that she forgets to actually care.

"Okay," I shrugged. I wasn't going to do it. "Are we done here?"

"I think you should go talk to the nurse."

The health room smells like cough drops, but I decided that this small surrender might help her feel she had done something for me. Maybe then she'd back off.

I let her win. "Okay."

She moved to let me out of my desk, and I reported to the nurse's office where I claimed a headache and was given permission to doze through science as well.

On my way to art, I bumped into Tommy Nealer. Literally, unfortunately.

"Hey!" he said, cracking me a crooked smile but refusing to look me in the eyes. "How's it going, Artemis?"

My throat tightened stiff around my voice. "Good." If I were just a little closer, I'd be able to smell him. *He smells so good.* My feet shifted, and I leaned forward a smidge, asking softly, "Are you going to Dylan's party tonight?"

But he turned to where his friend was calling him and stepped away before I could get close enough.

"Yeah," he responded, talking over his shoulder to me, waving that his friend should wait up. "My car's full, though, sorry."

He wasn't. He was headed down the hall already.

As an afterthought, he turned back.

"Hit up Amanda for a ride. Catch you later."

Gone.

I had been changed by my experiences but he hadn't. I dreamt and the universe split in two; two separate but touching realities running side by side; me the only person with one foot in each.

I caught up with Jason in math class. It was weird seeing him again after last night, and, when he smiled at me from his desk, Tommy's kiss burned against my lips.

"Hey." Jason smiled at me.

"Hey," I said, dazed, wondering what Tommy was doing right now. *What class did he have? That's right, P.E. Maybe he was doing push-ups.*

"Are you feeling better?"

"Yeah, I guess."

"I hear there's going to be a big party at Dylan Souza's house tonight. His parents are out of town. Are you going?"

"Not sure. I kind of feel like I've already been. And it wasn't great."

"What do you mean?"

I laughed and looked for something in his eyes. I couldn't find it. "Nothing."

# NIGHT FOUR

Some things were the same.

I got myself dressed, fussing for a bit over which shoes to wear. In real life I only have four pairs, so it didn't take me hours and hours to figure it out. When I was ready, I left through the front door. Any normal freshman would have had to lie and cheat and sneak to get to go to this party. How could a responsible parent allow a fourteen-year-old to stay up all night with a bunch of seniors and coolers full of beer? It would be forbidden. But not in my house. My mother was awake when I left, but she had sunk so deep into the couch that it wasn't worth the effort to get back up again.

Amanda had parked out front. She was a nice enough girl. After all, she allowed a measly freshman like me to roll with her to the party. It was a nice enough school, I guess. People didn't go out of their way to put you down because you were younger, or exclude you because you weren't cool enough.

But they didn't go out of their way to include you either. After acknowledging my presence with a quick nod, the three girls in Amanda's car fell back into their own conversation. I didn't know if they were talking about real people or people from TV. The names weren't familiar. I buckled my seat belt and kept my mouth shut.

At Dylan's house, I gripped a beer in my hand and leaned against the wall, sizing things up. Personalities softened in the alcohol, allowing my classmates' carefully erected defenses to crumble away beer by beer.

I heard Tommy before I saw him. He'd been drinking—heavily by the sound of it—and his alter-ego had come out to play. I didn't like Tommy The Destroyer. In fact, I hated him so much that I broke up with the real Tommy because of him. If only he wouldn't drink.

Tommy The Destroyer leapt onto the back of a chair, toppling it over onto a couple of his friends who used to be my friends, too.

"Hey! Watch it, man," one of them said.

Challenged, Tommy The Destroyer leapt on top of him, knocking him into the bookcase and then to the floor. He wrestled the beer out of his friend's hand and downed it in one swallow. "I don't watch anything. You watch out for me." He got up and reached a hand out to help his friend stand as well. They were laughing. This was how they played.

As soon as his friend was standing, Tommy got in real close, as if he had a secret to share. "Balls!" he howled, and five or six people around him took up the chorus.

"Balls!" they all cheered and downed their drinks.

I hate him. I really do. But I couldn't take my eyes off him.

"You suck, Tommy Destructo," I mumbled into my beer can, tipping it toward my lips to hide their movements.

I was still watching him when a skinny girl with long, black curls sauntered up next to me.

"He's cute, isn't he?"

She looked young, but that could have been the red plaid skirt and knee socks talking. *What is this, Halloween?*

"Huh?" I inquired.

"Tommy. He's super hot."

"He's an idiot." As if to prove my point, Tommy The Destroyer pulled a few books off the shelves and launched them around the room.

She giggled up an alluring noise. The males in the immediate vicinity perked up their ears.

"And he's so funny."

Okay, this girl was an idiot, too. She had these big, googly eyes, like a deer. Like a dumb deer standing in the middle of the road just staring into oncoming traffic.

"He's my ex."

"What?" She was listening to Tommy shout about balls. In her defense, it was hard for me to even hear myself over him.

I made a weird face and shrugged. There was a lot I wanted to say with that look. "He's a total dipshit," my face said. "Sure, he's hot and most of the time he's a really nice guy but then he turns into the asshole that you see before you. You don't want to get involved with a person like that. You'll never know who you're dealing with."

She, however, gleaned this from the look: "Should I like him, too? If you like him that must mean he's right to like. What do you think?"

And so she clicked her teeth at me and answered, "He's out of your league," before gliding over in his direction. Perhaps he smelled like gardenias. Delicious gardenias. She must have been unable to resist the grazing opportunity.

I watched her for awhile, throwing her head back when she laughed to reveal a long pale neck. Then I felt a little seasick and went in search of a second beer to settle my stomach and distract me from the icky courtship display.

With my second drink now in hand, I wandered down the hall and into the garage. A ping-pong table sat lonely and unattended in the center of the room while a pack of about a dozen guys crowded one giggly, jiggly junior in a corner.

"No, it wasn't with the stick shift. Guess again," she invited.

*Wasn't what with the stick shift? Oh. Gross.* I backed up into the hall again, right into Hayley Anderson. I don't have too many girlfriends, not since elementary, anyway, when you couldn't be friends with boys.

"Hey, Artemis. How's it going?"

Hayley talks to everybody. Back in third grade, we were the founding members of the Secret Scribble Society, an art club that met in the butterfly house. It was supposed to be just her and me and Sara, but she told everyone and by the end of the week all the girls and some of the boys in Miss Sollars' class were crowded into the little butterfly house taking etchings of leaves and the wings of dead butterflies.

I shrugged. "Okay."

"How's the big art project going?"

"Oh, fine. I didn't know you knew about it."

"The whole school knows about it. We're excited to see it. Well, some of us are excited to see it. Some of us are excited to skip fourth period. But, I'm excited to see it. You're so creative."

"Thanks."

"Have you seen Mike and Sara?"

"Uh, no. Sorry."

"I'd better go track them down. See you at school."

"See ya."

Alone again, I pressed my back to the hallway wall and tracked the development of Dylan Souza from a joyous naked baby in a sink to a thick-jawed near-man with a stupid grin and a football tucked under one arm. His parents had told a sad story with these photos, though I'm sure they couldn't have meant to.

In the living room, the big Dylan chugged a beer through a funnel and a short length of plastic hose. I looked again at the tiny, naked baby Dylan. Someone should have interfered.

That naked baby looked so happy there in his sink. I wish I could have jarred him, kept him safe from his future.

I don't have a wall like this in my house. It's like I dropped in on this life at age six, the day the latch on my lunch box broke and all the grapes bounced away along the sidewalk. I have no proof of my former innocence. Baby Artemis is lost to me. She is a ghost who vanishes the moment I look directly at her, laughing at me from just beyond the edge of my sight.

# DAY FIVE

Saturday was Prince's day. "Anything you want," I told him as I carved his waffle into tiny squares with a knife and fork.

"Butter and syrup in—"

"In each hole. I know, I know. I'm not a novice at this."

"That's how I like them."

He had his eyes fixed on my hands, and I could tell by the way he sometimes cringed that I wasn't cutting right on the middle of the ridges. I slid the plate to him and allowed him to pour an extra moat of syrup all the way around his waffle. He popped the squares into his mouth one at a time.

"So, Prince," I said, pouring syrup over my waffle carelessly and tearing it apart with my fork. "What do you want to do today?"

"Today is my day," he confirmed, nodding thoughtfully. "Carrots."

I waited for an elucidation that was not coming.

"Carrots," I repeated. "And what are we going to do with carrots? Eat them? Cook them? Stick them up our noses?

What?"

That was comic gold for a six-year-old if you ask me, but Prince only scrunched up his face and watched me quizzically. I was a creature he couldn't predict. Perhaps I was missing more than a few of my marbles.

"No," he told me gently. "There are no carrots. There are only their seeds. We have to plant the seeds into the Good Soil and then they will grow into carrots. They're for Walker." He might have been talking to a dumb child much younger than himself.

"Aren't there carrots at the store? If we walk into town, we can pick up a bag and have carrots today."

He sighed through a mouthful of waffle and finished chewing in his own time. He chose his words carefully. "No. Those are not good. Good Carrots are from their seeds." He reached into his pocket and pulled out a little white envelope folded over and over on itself. The only way to convince me of the obvious was to provide me with concrete evidence. I needed to see and touch to comprehend the difference between carrots and Good Carrots.

I held the envelope now, peering inside at the specks of seed. "Where did you get these?"

Again, Prince sighed. "Grandma."

"In the mail?"

"Yes."

"Grandma writes you letters?"

Prince stared at me but didn't respond. Wasn't I holding one of the letters Grandma wrote him?

I swallowed hard. "I didn't know Grandma wrote you letters."

I haven't talked to her in a long time. Not since our mother made me call her to tell her we weren't coming for Thanksgiving. She wouldn't even tell me why. I cried for weeks. Prince has no memory of that day, I'm sure. No memory of her, either. He was just a baby the last time we saw her.

Prince held a chubby hand out to me for the safe return of the Good Carrot seeds. "I need to make some more carrots. For Walker. You can fill the watering can."

I'd been granted a job. I must not be as hopeless as I felt.

Prince had already skipped off, out the back door and over to the far corner of the yard. From here, the car graveyard was out of sight. From here, the world looked alive. I guess I'd never realized that Prince had done all this. His garden seemed so accidental that I thought the earth had simply spit it up this way.

He knelt in the soil and poked quarter-inch deep holes in the ground with his pinky, depositing exactly two tiny carrot seeds into each one. He made swirls instead of rows, as if he could wrap this garden around himself like a blanket.

I carted the watering can over and placed it beside him. There were enough carrot seeds to bring the edge of the garden out an extra few feet. Prince scooted around in a circle, erecting a fortress around himself. When he had emptied the envelope, he smoothed the dirt over all the holes, encasing each pair of seeds.

He allowed me to do the watering, instructing me simply, "Just a little water because they're just baby seeds." With that, he turned his attention to the other plants.

A prickly vine skirted around one side of the garden. I turned to Prince and asked, "What's this? Should I water it, too?"

He barely glanced up. "That's zucchini. It's thirsty. You can give it water."

I did and then knelt beside Prince and watched his expert fingers twine another vine up and around a post.

"And what are these?"

He frowned. "That's green beans, silly."

Sure enough, they were. He lifted a branch so I could see the dozens of tiny, thin beans.

I pointed to another plant, a pretty red one with long, curly leaves. "And what's that one?"

Prince furrowed his brow when he saw what I was pointing at. "Artemis," he scolded, "that's a weed. Can't you tell the difference between the good plants and the garbage ones?" He ripped it from the ground, pulling up all of its spidery roots, and plunked it down in my hand. "It's garbage."

Like a dead creature, the weed flopped across my palm. But it wasn't dead, not yet. I felt sorry for it, sorry that it didn't have any value and deserved only to be thrown away. While Prince's back was turned, I slipped it inside my pocket. I'd plant it in the car graveyard when he wasn't watching.

"Hey," I chirped, hiding my transgression with a cheerful smile, "Do you think that if you planted the seeds from a bell pepper it would grow?"

"Grandma never sent me pepper seeds."

"We have an orange bell pepper in the fridge. Do you want to try to plant it?"

He looked to the house but didn't answer.

"Come on. It'd be like a science experiment."

"I like science."

"See? There you go."

Slipping his dirty hand into mine, Prince finally smiled at me. I'd gotten it right. I led him back to the house and held the screen door open for him as he tumbled into the kitchen. He was already digging through the fridge before I'd even stepped inside.

"Not my worst idea ever, I guess," I joked, elbowing my baby brother in the ribs.

"Where'd you put the pepper?" he demanded, burrowing farther into the back of the fridge.

"Let me look."

I pulled him out and rested him for a moment against one hip, the way I used to carry him when he was tiny. His legs still hugged my waist automatically, and his hands tightened into fists around my shirt.

"Aha!" I announced, pulling the bright orange vegetable out and placing it into Prince's outstretched hands.

He cheered and let himself slide down off my body and back to the floor, the pepper still held triumphantly above his head.

That was the moment that the front door opened and our father stepped into the house. I turned my head toward him and saw that he wore heavy boots and that his shirt was clean. When I looked back to Prince, he was gone. The pepper rolled into the hall, abandoned. This was Prince's day. He had no right to ruin it.

I opened my mouth to tell him to leave us alone but nothing came out.

My father's eyes darted around the room until they landed on mine. "What the hell happened to my Mustang?"

I skirted around the corner and receded into the depths of my room, submerging myself below a pile of clean clothes and magazines.

I could no longer see anyone; we were all but the breath and heartbeat of the house, which shook for us each time the screen door slammed.

Bang.

Our father sorted through what was left of his life here. He forced every drawer out of the dresser, their sides scraping against the inside frame. He turned them out and left them hollow like that on the floor.

Bang.

The closet door opened wide, bumping against the wall. Hangers flew from the bar in flocks. He gathered them together and ushered them out the door.

Bang.

The lamp next to the television teetered on its rim and then bonked over onto the floor, its bulb smashing into a thousand tiny pieces.

Bang.

The computer desk galloped down the hall, leaving a hole behind when one of its corners caught on the wall.

Bang.

The rip of the screen, quick like a bandage coming off my scraped knee, the sting of it lingering.

Bang.

The wind slid the loose end of screen back and forth across the half that was still attached.

The stillness lingered for half an hour before I ventured out from under the clothes. I tiptoed into Prince's room and peeked under the bed, but he wasn't there. I didn't open any of the closets.

The house was a war zone. Everything was everywhere. I found a dresser drawer in the kitchen sink and balled up socks scattered hazardously across the kitchen floor. The medicine cabinet had been opened, and its contents vomited down into the sink. Everything that had been in the hall closet was on the couch, and everything that had been in my parent's bedroom closet was on the hall floor. It seemed as if someone in a blindfold had sliced apart my life.

The pepper had been trampled. All that was left of it was a bright orange smear and a few broken seeds. For an hour I stumbled around the house, crying so hard I couldn't catch my breath. I threw my hands against the walls; I tore a discarded button-down shirt into slivers; I drew a bath, just to scream underwater. At one point, arms hugged tight around myself, I dug my nails so far into my skin that I scraped away long strips of myself.

Then I stopped. Just stopped. I didn't calm down, allowing my breath to tremble out in little gasps until it smoothed itself, tears stopping and starting again in rhythm. I just flipped a switch and turned from a raving lunatic back into a normal girl without even a hiccough to mark the transition.

I walked quietly into my mother's bathroom and cleaned my scratches.

# NIGHT FIVE

My skin still burned from the damage I inflicted on it. There was no side to lie on that offered any comfort. After an hour of rolling in circles on my bed, tangling and untangling the sheets, I got up, returned to the medicine cabinet, and swallowed a handful of ibuprofen.

That didn't seem like enough.

I took a few more, just to make sure. Then I stood at the mirror and waited.

After twenty minutes, my reflection blurred and my legs got all wobbly. A sudden exhaustion overcame me, and I stumbled back to bed where my body dissolved into a warm, numb, shapeless mass.

Closing my eyes and folding my hands across my chest, I listened to the slow, steady beat of my heart.

Then, silence. At first I couldn't move at all. If my heart were still beating, it would have upped the pace, pumped the adrenaline into every cell. I felt it, the cool panic, but distant, like an echo. Fear whispering death in my ear, I struggled against leaden eyelids, trying desperately to pry them open again despite the hermetic seals that had been formed. If I could just open my eyes, I'd be okay. I'd taken too many pills, but if I could just open my eyes everything would be fine. When at last I forced them open and sat up with a sudden burst of strength, I was in the middle of a jungle.

A man who I had never seen stood at my side.

"He is coming for you," he said.

My eyes sifted through the foliage. The man and I were in the middle of a clearing, surrounded by a forest that would return.

"Who?" I asked him, struggling to my feet.

"The tiger."

By the time I turned to ask him more, he had vanished.

The jungle was soundless. Even the sharp rise and fall of my own breath occurred in silence. Around me, dark green leaves rippled in circles though there was no breeze to disturb them. He was coming.

The tiger sprung out of the jungle so suddenly that there was no time for fear. He knocked me onto the ground, digging his claws deep into my arms, piercing through skin and muscle and bone. His face mere inches from mine, he let a thin strand of saliva slip down his lip and across my cheek. It smelled like meat and earth.

His black lips curled up to reveal the yellow swords that were his teeth.

"Not yet."

I pulled myself from the bed and vomited up everything that hadn't been absorbed. My face still pointed toward the bowl in the off chance that there was anything left, I raised a shaky hand to flush away the frothy, white bile that had bubbled out of me.

My face felt hot; I rested one cheek against the cold porcelain for a moment. The tiger's eyes still burned into the backs of mine. If I closed them I could see his face, so I forced them open and stared into the toilet water.

A baby giggled in the living room. *That can't be right.*

Again. I lifted my head and listened closely. *Sure enough.*

On unsteady legs, I approached the misplaced sound of a happy baby.

The open refrigerator door cast a dim blue light on the scene. It was my father. He had come back. He held a baby up by her chubby, pink hands, supporting her weight so she could stand on her own two tottering feet. When he brought her forward across the floor, her unpracticed gait forced her feet to slip out from under her, but he kept her body upright and safe from harm. He laughed and danced her around and around the room.

Nobody took her picture, though; nobody documented her existence.

I stepped forward, off the wall and out of the hallway, but, when I did, the scene disappeared and I was left alone in the blue glow of the fridge. I shut the door. The clock ticked steadily away.

"Artemis," my mother said.

I turned. It was dark in the house, but it looked like it was really her. High, high heels and all.

"Where are you going?" I asked.

"Go back to bed."

"But where are you going, Mom?"

She brushed by me, out the front door, letting the screen slam behind her.

I followed.

She was headed west, wearing a skin-tight leopard print skirt that did what it could to cover her ass and a short, short black leather jacket. My mother teetered a bit as she click-clacked down Locust Street, and I had to wonder how her heels stayed intact with the bend of each step.

Down toward town we went, and when the sidewalk flowed into a crosswalk with a red light, my mother strode unhindered through. A baby blue pickup in the middle of the intersection braked cleanly for her.

At the crosswalk, I stood with my finger on the button, pressing impatiently despite the fact that doing so does nothing to speed the change of the lights. I kept following her with my eyes until she turned right a block ahead of me and out of my line of vision.

I pressed the button in rapid fire. My mother was disappearing into the darkness. Press, press, press. *Come on.* The streets were deserted. I took a breath in, bolted across the road, and flashed down the sidewalk to the next light. By the time I reached the corner and turned the way I saw her go, I had already lost her. Regardless, my bare feet pounded farther down the street until I reached the next corner, where I paused to examine each of the four directions for clues.

Across the street on my left, a gaudy neon sign traced the outline of a martini glass into and out of existence.

Someone had set alight the grail-like beacon.

I stood in front of the bar until the cold from the sidewalk crept up through my feet and legs, into my chest, and then up into my head. But my mother didn't come out. Only when everything was numb and ice-hard did I turn around and head home.

# DAY SIX

THE LONG, WARM RAYS OF late afternoon sun pulled their fingers through my hair as I rested my face against the pavement. I stared into the west, toward the soft light of the sun, denying myself the pleasure of staring directly at it for more than a fleeting second. I'd glanced at it so many times that dozens of brown spots polka-dotted around behind my eyelids each time I closed them.

If I closed my left eye, all I could see was the sparkle in the pavement, glittering in its best impression of the sun. If I closed my right eye, all I could see was the sky. I like lying on the ground, especially when it's warm. It's like hugging the Earth. I should have been a snake.

I had woken up late; too late to see my mother stumble in at dawn; too late to picnic with Prince in the garden; too late to visit with Jason, who left a note and a photo when he stopped by this afternoon. I was dancing in the picture, dancing on a table with Megan and Amber. It was a good picture, but the girl in it wasn't me—not inside, anyway.

Jason tried to talk to me twice at Dylan's party, but each time he did I escaped, first onto the table with some of the cheerleaders, then out the front door. I walked all the way home just so I wouldn't have to turn him down.

A woman walking her dog stopped in front of me. "You shouldn't lie in the road," she reminded me. "You could get hurt."

"I am hurt," I told her, still blinking out the sky and the pavement in turn.

"Well, there you go," she snipped, pulling at her beagle's leash. They vanished around the corner.

She must have thought I was lying. I guess I was, sort of.

I went inside again once the sun was all the way gone and the pavement started taking away warmth rather than giving it to me. Prince was in his room. I couldn't see him but I could hear him—he had his big bucket of LEGOs out and he was tipping it over as slowly as his hands could move it. I moved to his doorway so I could watch, though I knew the process by heart.

He lowered the lip of the bucket steadily, if not microscopically, closer to the floor. At first, only a few of the plastic blocks shook loose and tumbled over one another toward the ground. Some made the jump prematurely, landing on the carpet before the bucket was all the way on its side, before the avalanche of tiny blue and yellow and red bricks came crashing—though always slowly—down into a pile on the floor.

With the bucket on its side, LEGO carnage oozing from its mouth, Prince danced around behind it on tip-toes, hooked his fingers under the groove along the bottom, and began to lift just as slowly as before.

The blocks tumbled out a few at a time, rising slowly into a mountain.

When he had the bucket forty-five degrees spilled (you could have put a protractor to this boy's consistency), and there were as many LEGOs on the floor as there were still in the bucket, he paused. He anchored his feet and took a deep breath. His shoulders trembled ever so slightly.

One final crash and the bucket was upside-down in his hands and the LEGOs were a mess all over the floor. Walker jumped straight up, kicked his legs out sideways from his body, and bolted beneath the bed.

Prince didn't notice, though. He stood in the center of the room, the bucket pressed between his chubby hands, fingers spread wide, a hint of a smile on his face. He could have been a sculptor the way he stood there, ogling all the possibilities that this unformed mess contained.

I drifted into the kitchen to start making dinner for the two of us—maybe three if our mother reappeared—but as I walked by the TV I discovered a hole in my father's orange plaid chair. He hadn't taken it with him. I wouldn't have either.

I stared at the hole for a long time, at first not sure if it was real. No, there was definitely a hole in that chair. I reached out to touch it but pulled my hand back again, in case the emptiness could spread to parts of me if I got too close.

My father's work boots lay abandoned near the chair. I strapped them on. They fit easily over the shoes I was already wearing, their cracked leather slipping off in uneven strips. I tied them as tight as I could, but there was no way to secure them. If I lifted my feet a couple inches off the ground, they'd release their tenuous grasp and fall off. So I had to shuffle into the kitchen, kicking any sock ball that dared to block my progression to the fridge.

With my father's boots and a can of Miller to protect me, I settled myself into the hole in the chair and pressed my beer into the cup holder my father had created on the right armrest through years of cramming his can down into that same spot.

I don't remember turning on the TV. Maybe it had been on all along. There was a basketball game in progress. I shouted at it, yelled for those dumbasses to pick it up. Shoot. Shoot, damn it, shoot.

Behind me, the freezer door opened, and Prince popped open a bag of frozen green beans. I didn't turn to check on him; I just let him eat his ice beans for dinner and tried my best not to slip out of that hole.

# NIGHT SIX

Tommy snuck in through my bedroom window the way he used to.

I would have slid the window shut after him, but the eerie glow of not one but two full moons caught my eye. They peeked out at the car graveyard from above the neighbor's hedges, no doubt gossiping about us the way our nosey neighbors sometimes do.

"I didn't know this was supposed to be a two-moon night," I said, lying on the bed next to Tommy and resting my head on his chest.

But he didn't speak.

I breathed him in and let my fingertips feel all tingly against the steady rise and fall of his chest. After a moment, he reached down and pulled my face up to his, pressing his lips against mine.

"Tommy."

I pushed him back an inch, but he quickly closed the space again.

This time I shoved him harder. To wake him up. "We broke up. Remember? You drink too much."

"Not all the time. I'm not drinking now."

He wasn't lying. I couldn't taste any liquor on his tongue. Not beer, not vodka, not anything.

"Artemis," he said, his voice soft and low like a far-away motorcycle. "Do you remember what you did? The other night at the party?"

"Nothing. I just waited for you. But you never came. You wouldn't talk to me, not in front of the others. Not anymore."

"You don't remember?"

"Why don't you just tell me? I don't want to play this game."

Instead of answering, Tommy pulled out his phone. I'd been tagged in a video. The picture quality was shit, and you'd never have been able to determine conclusively that it was me but for the white box around my head with my name in it.

I didn't remember taking off my shirt when I was dancing on Dylan's dining room table. But there I was.

"I took that at the party," Tommy sneered.

"What?"

"I put it up so everyone would know what a freak you are."

"How can you do this to me?"

He laughed, but just with his breath.

I pushed him out of my bed and slapped him as hard as I could, but my hand splashed off his face like water. Unfazed, he climbed out the open window.

Another Tommy paused beside me to place a sympathetic hand on my shoulder. "I'm sorry," he said. "You know I have no control over him."

"How would you know? You never even try. I think you'd better leave."

He climbed out the window, and I bolted through the house, out the front door, and down the street a half a block to where I could see the two Tommys walking away. "I think you forgot something," I screamed.

I waited for them to turn and look and, when they did, I plunged my hand deep inside me and tore out my still-beating heart.

They shook their heads. "It's not for me," they said.

Then they turned away, walked slowly up the hill and back into each other, leaving me there in the middle of the street holding my heart in my hand.

# DAY SEVEN

I WOKE UP TURNED THE wrong way, with my feet toward the open window and my head slipping off the bottom edge of the bed. Sitting up was out of the question. I felt like there was a butcher knife jammed into my skull, twisting, twisting, twisting. I tried to swallow some of the pain away, but my tongue was a wad of cotton so thick I couldn't close my mouth the whole way.

It was a dream. Of course it was a dream, but I don't remember opening the window last night. What else don't I remember?

"Where's my breakfast?"

I couldn't think about food. Even the word food made me feel sick.

"Artemis, where's my breakfast?"

"Can't you get yourself a bowl of cereal or something?" I sounded horrible, like someone drove a lawn mower across my vocal chords.

"No. I want an egg."

"Ask Mom."

"Mom's sleeping."

"So am I."

"Please make me an egg, Artemis. Please. And toast without burning it."

"I'm not feeling well."

"Maybe eggs and toast would make you better. You could make them with butter on them."

"Just wait a minute," I snapped. "I have a headache. Sometimes you're a real pain, you know that?"

That stopped him.

I slid out of bed and swam down the hallway into the bathroom. By the time I emerged to make Prince's breakfast, he was dressed and heading for the door.

"Hey. I thought you wanted an egg and unburned toast."

"You're going to make me be late for school," was all he said. It was five to seven.

☼ ☼ ☼

I WOULD HAVE CRAWLED BENEATH the covers and spent the day snoozing, but there were holes in my memory that I just couldn't account for. I needed answers. I had to go to school to get them.

I caught up with Amanda at lunch.

"Hey," I said, siding up to her in the cafeteria.

"Hey!" she answered, smiling.

"I need to ask you something."

"Sure. What's up?"

Amanda was a sucker for gossip. If anyone could fill in the blanks, it was her. "You know Dylan's party. It's just... I had this dream and I... Something's been bugging me. Like, maybe I'm forgetting something important, you know? I... Do you remember seeing anything, well, strange at the party?"

She squinted her eyes and turned her head ever so slightly to the side. She knew. She knew I was nuts. I shouldn't have said anything to her.

"Well, it was a wild party," she said at last. "There was a lot of strange stuff going on." No, she didn't know. I was still passing for normal. *I've got to calm down.*

"Anything you remember that stands out?" I tried.

"Well... Oh! Amber and Darren totally hooked up. And you know she's going out with Steve, so that's going to be crazy when he gets back into town tomorrow. And I saw Marina kissing Nick, Snyder not Reid, which I definitely saw coming. But WHOA anyway, you know? OMG."

This wasn't exactly what I had in mind. I stood there as Amanda ran through the list of new and scandalous hook ups. I tried not to tune her out, but her lips were flying so fast through all those names that I just couldn't keep up.

She would have kept talking, possibly forever, but I cut her off at an inhale.

"Did you see me at all?"

Her expression teased me. Now she knew why I was asking. She took on the air of my confidant and slipped me under her arm.

Keeping my lips pressed in a tight line, I held my breath, waiting to see if the topless dancing was real or dreamt.

"OMG. No! Who did you hook up with?" Her pigtails bounced up and down on her head like a pair of yellow springs.

"Um... No, it's not that." I couldn't say it. It was crazy. It was just a dream. Just a stupid dream about stupid Tommy. None of it was real, not Tommy, not the kiss, and certainly not the video. My brain had just made it up to scare me.

Shit. Why couldn't I let it go?

She slid her arm off my shoulder. There was nothing else to talk about, so why was I here? Then her eyes flashed again, and she covered her mouth with her hand before whispering to me, "Did you try the beer bong? I heard that Valerie totally puked all over herself when she did. I think that's crazy anyway. I mean, I could never do something like that. I'm a total lightweight, you know. I only weigh a hundred and two and I just couldn't drink that fast."

I shrugged and shook my head. This was a mistake. I needed out.

"I thought your outfit was totally killer," I told her, derailing her from the conversation.

"Aww. Thanks, Artemis. You're so sweet."

"Well, I've got to go. It was good talking to you."

"Totally. See you later."

We stepped away from each other and moved back toward our respective worlds. I was almost out the cafeteria door when she called me back.

"Artemis!"

I cringed.

"I totally remember. I did see something strange."

I did my best to look pleasantly surprised instead of horror-struck. "Oh?"

"Jerry."

"What?"

"Jerry, you know, that boy." She ushered me back and turned me in the direction of Jason. He was sitting at a table with a few friends, rolling a couple of large dice—rescuing damsels in distress and fighting orcs, no doubt.

"Jason?"

"Yeah. I saw him watching you when you were dancing with Amber and Megan. I think he likes you."

I turned away from him and shrugged. "You saw me dancing?"

"Girl. You have got some serious moves."

She would have said if I'd been topless. She would have said.

"You should go for it. He's cute."

He was cute. But cute like a puppy dog. A fleeting sort of cute.

"Tommy's long gone, you know," she reminded me.

"I know."

"He's a dick, too."

"He's sweet. And a good photographer."

"Tommy?"

I shook my head. "Jason."

"Go talk to him."

"I talk to him all the time," I said, but Amanda had left me there staring at Jason who looked up and waved.

I had no choice but to wave back and join him and the geek club.

"Hey, Artemis," Jason said. "Want to join in on the quest?"

"Absolutely not."

He made a grave face and looked me straight in the eyes, dead serious. "Whatever you do, don't allow yourself to have any fun."

"Oh, don't worry. I won't. Fun is the last thing I want." I faked a shudder. "I remember the last time I had fun. I still have nightmares about it."

He smiled. So did I.

"What are you doing after school today?"

I shrugged.

"Want to go see *Zorba the Greek*? It's playing tonight at the Central Theatre."

"That can't possibly be the name of a real movie. You're making that up."

"It's real, I promise."

"Maybe."

"I'll pick you up at six."

"Oooo!" Jason's friends chanted.

He crossed his arms. "Be cool. It's not like that."

Why did my stomach hurt when he said that? It was what I wanted him to say.

“I didn’t say yes,” I snapped, immediately regretting it.

“You don’t want to come? That’s fine, don’t worry about it.”

“What if I’m busy?”

“Then don’t come. It’s not a big deal.”

“What if I want to?” *What the hell is wrong with me?*

“Then come.”

“But this is not a date.” I smooshed the idea down on the table with the tip of my finger.

“Of course it’s not.”

“I mean, I know that and you know that. Just make sure your friends know that, too.”

He laughed and took the dice back. “I attack with my dagger,” he said, rolling.

“I’ll see you later.” I had to get up. I had to get out of there.

“Six, then?”

“Yeah, six.”

☼ ☼ ☼

Six couldn’t come soon enough. It’s not that I was particularly anxious to hang out with Jason or anything; it’s just that I had to get out of the house. I was suffocating in there. Prince had shut himself up in the closet with Walker. He still wasn’t talking to me since I snapped at him this morning. Well, except to tell me that I smelled like our mother. I took another shower, but the smell wouldn’t come off.

Jason knocked on my front door at exactly six. He’s so odd.

We hopped into the back of the minivan, and his mom drove us downtown. She let us out in front of the theatre, handed Jason a twenty, and told us to call her when we were done. We bought a couple of ice cream sundaes and sat in the creaky old seats. There was still a stage and a red curtain from when this used to be a real playhouse.

Only seven people emerged from their homes to view *Zorba the Greek* that evening. It made me feel sort of sad for good ol’ Zorba.

Jason kept his hands to himself and his mind wrapped up in the film. His gaze never strayed from the screen, and he laughed aloud at all the jokes, even the bad ones. I couldn't focus. It was such a weird movie. I must have been daydreaming when the girl died because it didn't make any sense. She was fighting and spitting one minute and the next her throat was slit and she was dead. Like nothing.

I paid attention again when the French woman died and all those ladies swarmed into her room screaming and grabbing her stuff. I know it was just a movie, but there was something so real about that moment. It's the way your friends joke, "If you die can I have your computer?" But they're not really joking. They really would like your computer if you were dead. And given the chance, would they strip everything from you the instant you stopped kicking and scratching and spitting?

# NIGHT SEVEN

She had been full of life, and I mean that literally. Everything my grandmother touched turned green and thrived. I hadn't seen her in ages, but I still had her face memorized. Sometimes, when I would wake up in the middle of the night after a bad dream, I would close my eyes and picture her and the monsters would retreat.

I could see her so clearly. There was no mistaking it. This was my grandmother and she was dying.

She lay in a bed covered in quilts that she had once made, surrounded by knickknacks collected from Italy and Grenada and Brazil and Zanzibar.

"You can't go," I pleaded. "You can't leave us alone with them."

She struggled for breath. "I can't stay. Your mother won't have it."

"But it isn't fair."

"Listen to me now. Stop crying. I have something important to tell you." She'd said those words to me before. In just that order. "I don't know when I'm going to be able to see you again. You need to be strong and take care of your brother. Make sure he grows up right."

"I can't. I don't know how."

She lifted a shaky hand to my shoulder. "No one else is going to be there for him. It's all you. He's your responsibility."

"I didn't want this."

"That doesn't matter. We don't get to choose these things."

Lifting her body, Grandma reached up and wrapped her arms tight against me. I knew that she was strong enough to make it. I could tell.

But her voice barely reached beyond her lips. "With your permission," she whispered, and she was gone with her next breath.

The screaming banshee-women flooded into the room, washing away every memory of my grandmother's life in their stream of skin and shrieks, leaving nothing for me to hold on to.

"Stop, stop, stop," I cried. But when they finally did, all that was left was an empty room.

Zorba stood in the corner laughing and laughing. His eyes caught mine and he said to me, "I like you."

"Fuck you, Zorba."

He laughed even harder.

# DAY EIGHT

PRINCE STOPPED DEAD IN HIS tracks when he saw me standing at the dismissal gate with the kindergarten moms. I motioned for him to come over, but he wouldn't do it. I'm not sure whether he was still mad at me for yesterday or whether he was simply surprised to see me. It didn't matter though; as soon as I pulled a fresh bunch of carrots out of my backpack, he came running.

"Carrots!" he squealed.

"With their tops on," I cheered.

"Carrots with their tops on! Yay!"

"I know it's not the same as Good Carrots, but it's going to be awhile before those grow."

"Walker is going to love them. Thank you, Artemis."

He wrapped his arms around my neck and kissed my cheek. On our way home, he slipped his hand into mine and chattered on about Josie's birthday and having to turn his color even though it was Andy who drew on the table with a marker.

The front door had been left open. It was a good thing that we didn't own anything of value. I opened the screen and followed Prince into the empty house.

"Walker! We brought you some carrots with their tops on!" he shouted in a singsong voice.

I pulled off my backpack and flopped down onto the couch, digging my history textbook out and opening it to the chapter on Japan.

"Walker," he sang again. "We brought you some carrots with their tops on!"

He walked around the whole house like that, yelling into each of the rooms.

"Artemis," Prince said from the hall. "Have you seen Walker?"

I closed the book.

Our father had ripped the screen in his rush to leave us. He had ripped the screen. How had I forgotten?

I jumped to the door. The tear ran from the middle of the screen down to the floor. It was easily big enough for a rabbit, even a big rabbit like Walker, to fit through.

"Check under all the beds."

"I looked there."

"Check in the closets."

"I did it."

"Check... Check... Check under everything."

But neither of us moved from the door. I stepped outside just as Prince started to cry.

*Do you call a rabbit like you would a dog? Do they recognize their own names?*

Wandering back and forth among the azaleas in our neighbors' yards, I shouted, "Walker! Walker!" until my throat ached.

When I couldn't shout anymore, I plopped down on the front steps and rested my forehead on my knees. I should have fixed the screen as soon as it ripped. I should have taped it up.

"What's wrong?"

I looked up to see Jason standing in front of me, a trumpet case in his hand. He must have come from band practice.

"Walker's gone." I rubbed my hands against my eyes, but they were still red.

Jason was all business. "Where haven't you looked yet?"

"Everywhere. I've looked everywhere."

"Well, let's look again. Two pairs of eyes are better than one."

He pulled me up off the porch and dragged me back into the street to start up the fruitless search once more.

From the sidewalk, one concerned Samaritan asked, "Did you lose your dog?"

"Rabbit," Jason and I answered.

He scrunched his eyebrows together. "Aren't rabbits nocturnal? Maybe you should look for him tonight."

I sighed. "They're crepuscular."

"What?"

"They're awake at dawn and dusk."

"Right, well, it's four-thirty."

"Yeah. I guess it is."

I thanked the man for his help, told Jason to go home, and slunk back into the house. There was nothing we could do.

At sunset, Jason returned uninvited. He held a box full of odds and ends in one arm and a ladder under the other. I stood in the doorway and stared at him, slowly chewing on a peanut butter and jelly sandwich.

When there was room in my mouth, I asked, "What the hell is all this."

Jason smiled and whispered, "Shhh... be vewy, vewy quiet. We're hunting wabbits. I have some ideas." He displayed his collection of junk for my examination. I opened the screen door and looked in his box. Carrots, apples, a pillowcase, a cat carrier, a ball of yarn, and an MP3 player.

An unattractive laugh gurgled up from my throat. "Who are you, MacGyver?"

"Who?"

"You should skip a little more school. You're missing out on some quality daytime reruns."

Jason shook his head and set the ladder up against the side of the house.

He was serious. "Come on," he said.

I didn't budge. I didn't cross the threshold to join him outside in Crazyville.

"Look." Jason pulled a picture out of his pocket. It was Walker. He was sitting in the garden, his mouth full of green beans.

Jason had written a note on the back.

*Dear Prince,*

*When Walker caught sight of your beautiful garden he decided right then and there that he had to experience it for himself. But don't worry. Your sister will bring him back safe and sound. That's what you have her for.*

I placed it on top of the TV. I'd read it to Prince later.

A part of me wanted to give up, but Jason's optimism was as contagious as the flu.

"Give me the string," he ordered.

I gave it to him, and he tied it to one end of a twig that he yanked off a pine tree.

"Give me the box, too."

"The box?"

"Yes, the box. And a carrot to bait it with."

Jason took the box, placed a carrot underneath it, and propped one end up with the stick, just like in those old Bugs Bunny cartoons. Holding onto his end of the string, he climbed up onto the roof. I followed him up with the rest of the junk. That's how I wound up sitting on my roof next to Jason Messenger, fishing for Walker.

Up there, in the long, slanting light of the setting sun, Jason shined a little bit like a superhero. Everything was going to be alright; we were going to catch Walker for Prince.

There was no room for doubt up on the roof.

Jason cut himself another piece of string and tied it to the handle on top of the cat carrier.

He'd already lowered it halfway to the ground when I stopped him. "Won't he just jump out the door. Wait, bring it back."

I tied another string to the door. We baited it with apple slices and lowered it to the ground. Opening and closing the door from ten feet above was harder than it looked. We spent the better part of a half hour perfecting the delicate art of lifting the carrier while simultaneously slamming its door closed.

I picked up the pillowcase. "What's this for?"

"I figured we could drop it on him."

"Oh," I said.

Just after the last arc of sun melted below the distant hills, Walker emerged. The two traps were ready to go. Jason and I held the quivering string ends tight in our sweaty palms as Walker hopped around and around. He saw the carrot under the box first. We didn't rush. We waited until he was all the way safely under. Slowly, I pulled the string, tighter and tighter, until... BAM! The box crashed down to the sidewalk trapping Walker cleanly inside. But as we headed for the ladder to collect our prize, Walker flipped the box up off himself and hopped a few paces away from it, happily munching on his carrot.

Jason wasn't about to let a little setback like that get him down. He was a professional. He immediately redirected his attention to the cat carrier. Walker was already sniffing around it, eyeing the apple slices greedily. As soon as he hopped inside, Jason hoisted the carrier up. I tried to work the string to get the door to close but I pulled it shut too hard, and it bounced back open again. Nothing to keep him contained, Walker hopped down to the ground, stuffing treats in his mouth and grunting rudely up at us.

I did the only logical thing I could do. I tried to drop the pillowcase over his head. I hit him with it, and he took a bite out of the fabric before retreating back into the garden for the remainder of the evening.

We would not see him again that night.

Above us, the stars began to emerge and I leaned down onto my back to watch. "The pillowcase was less inspired than the others," I said at last.

We laughed so hard our tears rolled down the roof.

# NIGHT EIGHT

In the middle of the night, I went outside again to snoop around for Walker. Large, unruly leaves tumbled off the fence; they had become disobedient in the years we had lived at this house not tending them, and they invaded the yard erratically. We didn't have a garden, we had a jungle.

I had neglected to put on my shoes. Outside, the ground prickled against my feet, but I wouldn't let that stop me. I wasn't going to let Prince down.

Twice I heard a rustle beside me and turned my head to see a brown shadow leap away into the darkness just beyond my reach. It was comforting to know that Walker was sticking around, even if he was proving impossible to capture. It was a little sad, too. If I were to escape, I would hop farther away.

The stars flickered in the clear night sky and a thinning half-moon rained a silver light on the yard, but it was too dim to see much more than colorless shadows. I lifted the droopy leaves of the squashes up to reveal countless hidden burrows.

"Walker? Are you in there?" I whispered into each one.

He didn't answer.

After an hour, I moved into the center of the car graveyard where I could watch the slow spiral of the Milky Way above me. Lost in the sky, I stopped thinking about Walker and Prince and my mother and my father and Jason and Movie-Star-Kisses-Tommy and Miss Gonzales and the man who told me I had spunk, and I just stood there. I stood between the Mustang and the Viper, both frozen in place forever on top of their cinder blocks, and I banished the whole world.

Stars filled my eyes. I don't know how long I stayed like that. It could have been hours.

The sound of my name brought me back.

"Artemis," came the call, soft and faraway.

By the time I turned around, the garden had erupted in violent, untamed growth. "Artemis," I heard again, and this time I recognized the voice.

"Prince! I'm coming."

I plunged into the heart of the garden where monstrous leaves reached down to scratch at my cheeks. I shoved them away with clumsy hands. Under the canopy, the darkness was complete. I struggled to see anything more than an arm's length away. I was lost from the moment I broke through the foliage. How in the world could it have grown so enormous?

My heart pounded a hole out through the front of my chest trying to escape, to retreat back to safety under the covers. I steadied it with my hand and moved forward despite my better judgment. *It's only the night playing a trick on me. It's the same garden that it always is.* I swallowed the numbing terror that broke in waves across my body, leaving its cold sea spray on my forehead.

"Prince," my unsteady voice cracked out. There was no power behind my call; the word evaporated the moment it left my lips. I tried again. "Prince." This time it was nothing but a creaking rocking chair of a whisper.

A crackle in the leaves ahead made me freeze in place. I was being watched, I was sure of it. Something was waiting for just the right moment to pounce on me.

I swear I heard the low growl of a tiger, somewhere out there in the darkness.

My legs ached to run, but I refused to let them. I had to find my brother. He was too small. This place would devour him.

"Prince!" My voice burst out as a sharp scream.

There was a rustling in the bushes next to me. I moved toward it, into the fear.

"Prince! Prince!" Hot tears rolled down my cheeks as my hands tore at the leaves. I ripped up the mutant carrots and green beans and lettuce. I laid waste to the garden.

Prince placed a gentle hand on my wrist, putting an end to the madness. His short fingers couldn't even make it all the way around.

"What are you doing?" His voice was soft and disapproving; he frowned at me in grown-up disappointment.

I wrapped my arms around him and pressed him into my body with all my strength. "You're lost. I'm here to rescue you. I'm here to take you home."

He rested his cheek against my shoulder and said in a wise, sad voice, "No. It's you who's lost." He pushed me away a little, his arms hanging loosely around my neck, his eyes clear and bright in the darkness. "I think you should leave now. This place isn't for you."

He pushed me all the way out of the garden, back under the sky, and turned and chased after Walker, the leaves closing around him.

"Wait. You need me," I pleaded, but he was already gone.

He didn't need me. No one did.

Above me, Mars glowed red in the dark emptiness of space. It tugged on me like a magnet, pulling so hard that it lifted me up off the ground. I gathered speed, free-falling into the sky until the details of the planet emerged. Its valleys sunk low in my vision, and its mountains reached up to impale me. Mars grew bigger and bigger until it saturated all the space within my pupils.

Were someone to look at me then, I would have had red Mars for eyes.

☽ ☽ ☽

THE SOUND OF KNUCKLES RAPPING against my window nearly made me jump straight up out of my skin. I flew off the bed and faced the closed blinds a few feet in front of me.

Again: Knock, knock, knock, knock.

Who does this? Who comes to people's windows in the middle of the night? Shaking like a jack hammer, barely able to breathe, I started to reach for the string to raise the blinds. Then I thought better of it. What if it were a kidnapper? Or a murderer? It better not be a murderer. I don't need that kind of shit. But then, if it were a murderer he probably wouldn't knock first, he'd just sneak in through the unlocked back door. Unless he wanted to trick me into coming next to the window, so he could snatch me away as soon as I opened it, leaving behind no finger prints. But if that—

Knock, knock, knock, knock! More urgently.

My hand returned to my side, and I bolted from my room, grabbed the rolling pin from the bottom drawer, zipped out the back door, catching the screen, and tip-toed around to my bedroom window.

Jason had his nose against the glass and his hands cupped around his eyes. He was fogging up the window with his breath. I whacked him in the arm with the rolling pin.

"Ow!"

"What the hell are you doing?"

"What the hell are *you* doing?"

"I'm knocking some sense into you. Who does this? It's the middle of the night. Are you out of your mind? I thought you were a murderer or something."

"Whoa!" He held his hands up in surrender. "Lots of people do this; it's in all the movies. No, I'm not out of my mind, thank you. And, if I were a murderer, why on earth would I knock? Wouldn't I just sneak inside, and, well, murder?"

I was furious, so furious that I quite literally stomped my foot on the ground. "What do you want?"

He smiled at me from a beam of moonlight. "Take it easy. I need your help with something. In all the excitement I forgot to tell you about it, but it kept nagging at me. I couldn't sleep. Can you come out and play?"

"Are you completely insane? What time is it?"

"One-thirty."

"What? No I can't come out and play. It's the middle of the goddamn night."

"Why not? Is someone going to be up all night worried about you?"

I hit him with the rolling pin again, aiming for the same spot.

He cringed. "Ow! What was *that* for? Look, you're the only one who can help. I really need you on this one. Will you just come with me?"

That was the moment that my mouth betrayed me. I may never trust it again. "Fine," I hissed through clenched teeth. "Let me get some shoes."

Back inside, I pulled on my oldest pair of tennis shoes, single knotting them defiantly. I pushed open the door and slunk outside. Jason put a hand on my wrist, tugging softly.

I yanked my hand away. "What do you need?"

He didn't answer. He just ran straight across the street away from me.

My legs chased after him.

Through the neighborhood we flew, up and over fences, around flower beds and vegetable patches, across carefully manicured lawns, through all the back ways to get downtown. We hopped a red brick wall into the alleyway behind a bakery. I dropped to the ground so hard it stung the bottoms of my feet.

"We're here," he panted, breathless.

"You've got to be kidding me."

"I know, right? My mom and I stopped here for breakfast before school. I can't believe that someone would do this. I just don't understand people."

*I don't understand you,* I wanted to scream. *Why would you drag me out of bed in the middle of the night to bring me to a stinky alley that's shouting FUCK YOU at me in four foot tall letters? What's wrong with you?*

But I didn't say any of that. I just stood there staring at the graffiti that arched across the back door of the bakery.

Catching his breath, Jason continued, "We have to fix this."

He smiled and handed me a can of blue spray paint. His backpack was stuffed full with every color.

# DAY NINE

In two days it will be both the night of the senior prom and the first day of spring break. I'm convinced that the teachers look forward to this more than the students. They think that we don't pay attention, that we can't really see them, but I do. I see the way they flinch and rub their temples under the endless barrage of inane questions. I notice that the lessons grow more mechanical and unconscious as the hours drag on, day after day. We are all on autopilot, asleep at the helm.

Today in English, our teacher handed us pages from a coloring book. We listened to an old tape (played on an actual tape player) of some long-dead British actor with far too much vocal inflection recount the tales of Odysseus as we filled in the coloring book pages with cobalt and chartreuse and mellow yellow crayons.

My classmates dozed or texted with friends. My English teacher circled absently around the room. Only the actor on the tape seemed keenly enthralled by this moment, and he was dead.

Bored, I spilled the box of crayons onto my desk and super-imposed an image of my own on top of a scene of Aphrodite skipping off on her husband with her brother. My picture was a bird on fire. It was crying cornflower blue tears as hungry flames licked at its shoulders. But it wouldn't be able to cry hard enough to put out the inferno and it knew it was dying.

I raised my hand. "Mr. Bruner, can I go to the bathroom?"

He looked at the clock and shrugged his shoulders. Close enough for me.

In the bathroom, the girl from the party, the one with eyes for my ex, hung over the sink, flooding it with an open faucet of her tears.

"Hey," I started, with no real follow up to that thought.

She sobbed loudly, unembarrassed by my intrusion.

"Fuck him!" she screamed at the mirror, slapping her reflection on the forehead.

"Oh." I started to back away. "I can just use the bathroom in the B wing. You want to be alone."

She pinned me to the wall with her gaze, her make-up a disaster at mime college. "Why are men such fucking pigs?"

I shook my head. "Yeah… I—"

"I mean, aren't I good enough for him? How does he get off treating me like that? That fucking pig!"

This conversation really wasn't for me, I was just the one standing close enough to hear, the anonymous audience.

Unafraid of superstitious mumbo-jumbo, she smacked her hand against the mirror again. And again. And one more time for good measure, screaming "fuck" with each hit.

But she didn't crack the glass.

"Ow." She gritted her teeth and peeled her hand from the mirror, cradling it as if it were broken. It was bright red. Distracted by the pain on the outside, her tears stopped. She'd turned them off at the source. "I met you at the party, didn't I?"

I nodded.

"Let me give you some advice. Don't ever go out with Tommy Nealer. He's a total asshole. Get me a piece of toilet paper."

I did as I was told.

"Just tell me that all men aren't like that. Tell me that there's still some fucking chivalry left in the world." She snatched the paper from me and used it to dab her eyes from below in an attempt to not smudge what makeup she had left.

"I think Tommy's just like that."

"Aren't there any good guys around?"

I shrugged, shook my head.

"If that pig ever asks you out, you tell him no, you hear."

"Yeah. I don't think that's going to happen, though."

"That asshole. No fucking sense of decency." She rearranged her hair and wiped up the shimmering trail of tears flowing from her eyes to her chin. "And Melanie Suarez is a bitch, too."

I shrugged a sort of what-can-you-do shrug. "Bitch," I parroted.

"You're okay," she told me.

I didn't feel okay. I watched my reflection suspiciously.

"What's your name?"

"Artemis."

"Cool name. Like the books."

"Yeah. Just like that."

"My name's Nina. I'll see you around, Artemis."

She had pulled herself from a cocoon of despair and exited the bathroom looking again like a functioning human being. I wondered if I could have made a transformation like that.

My focus returned to the mirror where I studied my reflection for clues. My hair is too stringy. My eyes are too far apart. I smashed a finger against my nose. No, that's worse.

The bell announcing the end of class woke me from my trance. I had forgotten where I was. With no desire to brave

Miss Gonzales, I decided to go to art a couple hours early. After all, my project was going up right before lunch. I should start getting ready. If Mr. Bowman wasn't paying close attention, I could sometimes hide out behind an easel for hours.

Mr. Bowman had his second period class putting the final touches on the tombstones.

"What do you think?" he asked without looking at me.

I nodded, "Looking good."

"What class are you supposed to be in?" For dramatic flair, he raised one eyebrow.

I shook my head. "You know, some of the experts are saying that children thrive when they're given the opportunity to pursue their passions."

He wasn't going for it. "Whose class are you cutting, Miss Cato?"

"We could take this opportunity to go over some of the last minute details for the project. It goes up in a couple of hours."

"Math or history?"

"History."

"You know that Miss Gonzales doesn't like it when I let you cut her class."

"Come on, we're not doing anything. We're just watching a movie."

"What movie?"

"*Seven Samurai.*"

"Really?"

"I have no idea."

Taking a deep breath and pretending to stroke the beard he didn't have, Mr. Bowman considered rescuing me from the dragon of second period history. I did my best to look like a damsel in distress.

"You're lucky that I'm feeling generous today. I'll write you a pass so you can miss the first ten minutes. But that's all. Come with me. I want to show you something." He steered me toward the door shouting, "Keep painting," over his shoulder. A wrecked Mustang sat on the front lawn. Mr. Bowman had poured stage blood all over the hood. Or he'd slaughtered a pig on it. It was hard to tell from twenty feet away.

My hands started shaking. "What the hell is this?"

"Drunk driving accident."

"But. Why this?" It was the same paintless rust color as the one at home.

"We talked about this. I thought you liked the idea."

"Not this car."

"Well, we're in it now. My brother won't be towing it away until tonight. Sorry, Artemis."

"But not this car." He wasn't getting it. It wasn't a car, it was this car. It was this car that made the whole school smell like the car graveyard forever. "It's too close," I tried to say, but I couldn't. I couldn't explain it.

I sat down in the dirt and cried.

"Hey. It's going to be okay. It's going to be great. They're going to love it. And what's more, it's going to make this town safer. This is going to make a difference."

"It doesn't matter."

"Hey. I'm sorry. I thought it was what you wanted."

"Not this car."

"Come on back. You can rest in my office until you feel better."

Inside, I curled up on the raggedy couch and fell into a soft, dreamless sleep.

My art class arrived an hour before lunch. I helped dress them up in garbage bags, smeared fake blood all over their faces, and arranged them as the dead. Mindy Ellerton put on a beautiful, cream-colored gown and climbed through the broken windshield of the Mustang. She died like that on the hood, a line of blood across her forehead. Her boyfriend was the driver. He covered himself with blood and smashed himself across the steering wheel. I died on the grass amongst the tombstones. We all closed our eyes, then Mr. Bowman placed empty liquor bottles all around us.

We stayed dead for a half hour as our classmates hesitantly walked through our living piece of art. Mr. Bowman read the names of former students, the same names that arched across the tombstones, the names of those who'd died in drunk driving accidents. Over the years, we'd lost quite a few. Other teachers came forward to share stories about friends they had lost. The principal read a poem about a dying girl's last thoughts. A group of cheerleaders standing near my body sniffled audibly.

Mr. Bowman took the mic again. "You may be wondering why we're wearing trash bags. Of course, the first thing you'll notice is that they look like body bags, but it's more than that. Our message is simple: drinking and driving is effectively throwing your life away. You are not worthless. You are not garbage."

In the sunshine, I licked some of the blood from my lips. It tasted like cherry syrup, like a sugar rush at an amusement park, like the opposite of death. It was hot inside that bag. I cracked my eyes open. Mr. Bowman had placed an empty bottle of vodka in my hand. My mother's brand.

Jason placed a white rose on my dead body and then knelt down beside me.

"I thought of something."

"I'm dead," I hissed, trying not to move my lips.

"I know but just listen. I figured out how to catch Walker."

"No."

"No, listen. We take an apple, right? And cut it into little pieces. Then—"

"Not now. I'm busy." I squeezed my eyes shut again.

"No, listen. Then we take the pieces and make a trail back into the house. Walker will hop right inside as he eats them."

"Jason, that's not going to work."

"It will. Hundred percent."

"It won't."

"It totally will. He'll eat the apple and hop along right into the house. It's perfect."

"Jason. I don't want to talk about this right now. I'm supposed to be dead."

"I know, but it's going to work. We can—"

"It's a stupid idea. Go away."

"You've been taking grumpy pills again."

"Leave me alone."

"I like your project. When did you put tires on the Mustang?"

"It's not mine."

"It looks like yours."

"It's not, okay?"

He was quiet for a moment. "It's going to work," he said at last.

With my eyes still closed, I swung the empty vodka bottle at him but I missed; the bottle only swished through empty space. When I opened my eyes, he was gone.

The art class waited until the entire student body had left before we came back to life and took the project down.

# NIGHT NINE

JASON CAME OVER AT DUSK even though I told him not to bother. He placed a hand on my shoulder and, for once, I didn't shake it off.

"It's going to be okay," he said, and I foolishly believed him. "Hey, Prince! You know what today is?"

Prince had his mouth full of cold cheese sandwich. He shook his head.

"Today is the day that your sister is going to get Walker back for you. What do you think of that?"

I think that Jason expected Prince to jump up and down or cheer or smile or something, but he only nodded gravely. *She'd better,* he seemed to say.

We cut an apple into little squares and made a trail all the way from the backyard to the front door to Prince's bedroom. We even propped open the screen with a pile of books, in case Walker didn't remember about the hole.

We waited. And waited.

And waited.

But Walker never came.

"I'm sorry," Jason said on his way down the steps. "I really thought it would work."

"You need a little more practice at this whole superhero thing."

I let the screen door close and watched Jason walk out into the starless night, his hands stuffed into his pockets, his head down.

Behind me, Prince sat on the couch staring into the shadow under the TV. I sat down next to him.

"I'm sorry, Prince."

He sighed but didn't lift his eyes to meet mine.

"Come on. It's going to be alright."

I placed a hand on his shoulder, but he wiggled out from under it.

"Look. I didn't lose your rabbit, okay."

He didn't say anything.

"You should have kept a better eye on him. It's your own fault. Not mine."

"You said." He whispered so softly I could barely hear him.

"It's not my job. I can't do everything."

"You said."

"It's not my damn job, Prince! I'm not the one who let him run around the house whenever he wanted. Maybe this will teach you to look after your things better."

He took a sharp breath in, as if he might scream.

But he didn't. His eyes shimmered and two streams of silent tears escaped.

I didn't want to look at him. "When are you going to grow up and stop being such a baby?" I screamed, storming into my bedroom and slamming the door behind me.

☽ ☽ ☽

It was still my bed—it was still my room—but many centuries had passed. Most of the roof had crumbled away.

Most of the walls, too. I lied on my back, dressed in thin pajamas, and made finger trails in the dust on the sheets. I licked cobwebs off my face, tongue flicking like a chameleon's. I watched the clouds gather overhead, heavy, ready to go. Only the orange-striped wallpaper was still intact. At least, it was on the parts of the walls that remained standing.

I heard her before I saw her and smelled her before I heard her. She had a complicated smell, like damp earth, rain, and smoke. A balance of growth and decay; a corpse buried under a pile of lilies.

I sat up in bed, sniffing the air, feeling hunted.

"Yoo-hoo." Her voice was that of a bell hit with a stick wrapped in cotton. It fell short somehow. Maybe I wasn't hearing all of it. "Yoo-hoo."

"Hello? Who's there?"

"Over here, silly."

I turned toward the sound and, seeing nothing, kept turning all the way around until I was right back where I started. It made her laugh.

"No, no. Over here."

I turned the other way. Nothing.

"Down here. No, here. No, to the left. There. Do you see me now?"

I didn't. "No."

Her sigh had the hint of a snarl in it. "Well, you're looking straight at me."

I couldn't have been. There was nothing in front of me but papered wall.

"Come closer," she purred, luring me in. "That's it. Just keep coming."

I crept slowly toward the wall.

"That's it. Right. Here."

She shook the orange bars hard, wiggling the wallpaper and sending me flying back onto the bed in the middle of the room. Still, I didn't see her, not really. She was an emptiness with edges, like someone had taken a pair of scissors and cut a hole in the world.

"What are you?"

She slinked along the wall, passing behind the darker bars as if in a cage. "I'm your shadow."

"No, you're not."

"Look down. Do you see your shadow at your feet?"

"No."

"That's because I'm over here." Her hands reached around the edges of two of the bars, blacking them out.

"How did you get free?"

"That doesn't matter right now. We have more pressing concerns."

"We do?"

"Prince."

"What about him?"

"She has him."

"Who?"

My shadow, or whatever it was, tugged at a corner of the wallpaper, ripping it down toward her. "Look through here."

It wasn't wide enough to see through, not without putting my face right up to it. I hesitated in the middle of the bed, struck by the childish notion that the floor was made of lava.

"Look," she ordered. "You don't have forever."

I slipped down, down onto the lava-floor and did as she said, pressed my cheek against the wall like she wanted me to.

There they were, Prince and the witch. She had him on her lap, one spindly arm hugging his shoulder, the other holding little candies in front of his face. He was eating right out of her palm.

"You see?" my shadow whispered.

"Open it wider."

"No. Not yet."

"Yes, do it now. Rip it open. I'm coming in."

"No. You can't come in without a sacrifice."

I knew that. "A sacrifice?"

"Walker."

"Walker?" I knew that, too.

"Go and get him." Her voice thudded against the inside of my head.

"But I don't know where he is."

"Is there nothing but a cold wind between your ears? He's in his burrow in the garden, you stupid girl. Now go get him and bring him here."

"But," my voice faltered.

"Go get him." Her tone darkened.

"How?"

"Climb down his burrow and drag him out."

I didn't dare tell her that I would never fit down a rabbit hole. She wouldn't like to hear that. I flew over the crumbling wall and out into the garden.

The burrow wasn't well hidden, not anymore. I dove into it like diving into a pool the first time, before you're all wet, when you know that the shock of cold is going to take your breath away but you do it anyway. I dove straight into that hole and squeezed and strained and dragged myself deeper and deeper into the earth.

It should have been dark underground. It wasn't dark at all.

I tumbled out of the narrow passageway into a main room that opened wide and tall, not tall enough for me to stand, but tall enough that I didn't feel like I was being buried alive.

At the fireside, Walker sat in a chair with his legs crossed and his back to me. Without turning, he began to speak. "So, you've come for me then?" He had a man's deep voice. It sort of suited him.

"It's for Prince."

"Isn't it always?"

"Isn't it."

"Well, I suppose we'd better get going then." He stood on two legs, stretched his arms above his head, and turned to face me. His nakedness struck me as odd, odder than his hearth, him standing there on two legs, or even his human voice. If only he had a little vest or a hat. I should have made him a hat when I had the chance.

I lowered my eyes. "You'd come with me? You'd give up your freedom just like that?"

"How would you go? Kicking and scratching and spitting? No, my child. When your time comes, you walk to meet it."

"I'm sorry."

"She's lying to you, you know."

"Who?"

"The smoke pixie. Who else?"

"She said she was my shadow."

"She's lying."

"I'll think of something."

"You won't think of it fast enough."

"We have to try, Walker."

"Yes, I suppose we do."

"I'm sorry."

He grunted and came to me so I could carry him out of his burrow, holding his feet with my hands so he couldn't kick and hurt himself.

Inside the ruins of my bedroom, my shadow paced back and forth in the wall. "About time," she hissed at me.

"Sorry."

"Get in." She pulled at the paper a little more, making a crack that Walker and I could just slip through.

When I stepped out onto the other side of the wallpaper, the witch turned her head toward me. Her face was veiled. I couldn't see if she had eyes or not. I hoped she did. She scraped her long nails against Prince's scalp, and he moved into it the way a dog does.

"So nice of you to join us." I'd heard her voice before but I couldn't place it.

I sucked in a shaky breath and scooted forward. "Give me back my brother."

"Give me the rabbit," she countered.

Walker kicked against my hands, but I held him fast. A few tears wiggled loose and dripped down my cheeks, making little rivers to my chin. I'd wanted to be so much braver.

"Come closer, dear."

"You'll let Prince go," I said, letting even more tears escape.

"He will be free to make his own choices. You all will. Now, come here. Give Walker to me."

I handed over my prisoner. She took him by the ears and slowly stood, letting Prince drop from her lap onto the cushy pillows atop her throne.

Without warning, the smoke pixie grabbed me by the arms. It burned where she touched me, so hot it made me scream. But pain, like anything, is something you can get used to.

The witch was smiling beneath her veil. I could hear it in her voice. "Good girl. And now..."

With Walker still dangling by the ears, she glided across the floor to a small table. On it, there was a large, golden chalice and a long, crooked knife.

"Prince, Prince! Come here! Prince, come to me!" I screamed, but he kept his eyes on his bunny.

The witch muttered to herself in a language I didn't understand.

"Prince, come here! Prince!"

Prince sat transfixed. The pixie didn't loosen her searing hands one bit.

"Look away, Prince. Look away!"

He wouldn't turn.

She lifted the knife. Seeing it, Walker kicked. He kicked, and I struggled against the smoke that held me back. This was my fault. This was all my fault.

Then, Walker kicked the air so hard that he broke his back. It didn't stop her. She plunged the knife into his heart and let him bleed into the chalice. Once the last of him had drained away, the witch put his body and the knife on the table and took the cup in her hands.

It wasn't for her. She carried it to Prince and let him have it all.

He smiled at me then, for the first time since Walker ran away, his lips Kool-Aid red.

# DAY TEN

The walk home from school was awful. It was one of those days where the sun and the wind are at war and you're stuck in the middle, burned to a crisp and flash-frozen, one after the other after the other. There was no comfort. If I took off my hoodie, my arms turned into icicles. If I kept it on, I sweltered.

Things didn't improve when, sweat dripping down the back of my neck, I opened the front door. My mother was back. She cradled Prince in her arms and rocked him back and forth as he sobbed.

"Shh, baby, shh. It's gonna be alright. Shh, shh."

She kept cooing to him as she turned her dagger-sharp eyes to me.

I dropped my backpack on the floor and took off my sweatshirt, using a sleeve to wipe my neck.

"How could you do this to my baby boy?"

"What?"

"You let his bunny run away."

"I did not. Walker got out through the broken screen. Dad ripped it."

"It's your job to keep him happy, to protect him from shit like this. Shh, shh, baby, shh."

"It's not my job."

"You let him down. You let him down in the worst way. You're his older sister, for fuck's sake. You're supposed to be there for him."

"Where were you?"

"I had to leave work early to pick him up from school. He spent the whole morning crying. You let him go to school with his heart all broken. Didn't do a damn thing to make him feel better."

"That's not… I… Prince, you know—"

"I hate you, I hate you," he wailed.

"I don't even wanna look at you." My mother barked, turning away to feed Prince more comforting words.

"It's not my fault."

"Get the hell out of my sight," she screamed, launching a half-full can of beer at me. It splashed against the broken screen door.

"You want me out of here? Fine. You got it."

I stormed into my room, grabbed a few changes of clothes and stuffed them into the sidecar of my motorcycle. I was gone before the screen door slammed shut.

Eighteen miles out of town, I eased the bike onto the shoulder. Something wasn't right. I checked the gas. The tank was three quarters full. I used the hem of my shorts to clean the dipstick, but there was plenty of clean oil as well. Radiator wasn't overheating. Brake fluid was fine. I walked all the way around that bike and looked at everything, inside and out, but nothing was wrong. The problem was the rider.

I folded my arms tight across my chest and followed the highway out into the west with my eyes. I took off my helmet and shook my hair loose. I scraped the grime from my orange safety goggles. Finally, I pointed the motorcycle in the opposite direction and went back for him.

I didn't bother to park, I just stopped in the middle of the street and tromped across the lawn to the front door, almost pounding it down when I knocked.

"What are your plans for spring break?" I shouted. I must have looked like a thug in my helmet and goggles, yelling at him on his own front porch.

Jason's mouth dropped so far open that the crackers he was munching nearly slipped back out. "Uh... tomorrow I'm supposed to go see my dad in Salinas."

"Come with me instead."

"What? Where?"

"West."

"West? West where?"

I shook my head.

"Have you lost it?"

"It's possible."

"Why don't you come in?"

"I can't. I just need to get out of here. Just come with me. Please, I don't know how to do this. Just come, Jason. You can leave whenever you need to. I'll buy you a bus ticket home. I just need to go. Just... just..."

"Hold on."

He closed the door softly and reemerged a few minutes later with a backpack crammed so full the zipper was bursting.

"You'll need a helmet," I said, and he went around to the side yard to collect his electric blue bicycle helmet.

"Can we walk the motorcycle around to the corner? I don't want my mom to wake up from her nap and look out the window to see us riding off into the sunset together. She might worry. You know how mothers are."

"You don't walk a motorcycle." I was already straddling it.

Without a moment's pause, Jason Messenger strapped on his stupid-looking helmet. "Let's go then."

He slipped onto the bike behind me and hugged both arms around my waist. He wouldn't fall off if he wasn't holding me, but he didn't know that.

Everything was in place now. The 100cc engine roared to life and we rode away, straight into the sinking orange sun as fast as my wheels would turn.

# PART TWO

# NIGHT TEN

As the miles slipped away behind us, the pain of that afternoon—and a hundred others just as unbearable—began to relax its grip on me. Speed was not on our side. Impatient motorists huffed and puffed around us in complete disregard of the solid double-yellow line dividing the highway. Where we could, we rode on the shoulder, smiling and waving to the people who, apparently, had to be wherever they were going ten minutes ago. Some of them waved back, just not with their whole hands.

The road plowed on in great loose loops around the mountains. Here and there, dots of snow clung on stubbornly, winter's goodbye kiss. But the snow had already lost both its color and its consistency, like the last few sips of a Slurpie when the syrup comes up your straw too fast and too sweet and all the beautifully layered colors have mushed up into an indefinable brown. Dots of silver stone glinted on the hills, too—brought here from Canada and abandoned when the glaciers retreated. It always made me smile to think of glaciers retreating, as if they'd all of a sudden shouted "Run away!" instead of simply melting into water and finding their way down to the sea. Around and around the hills we rode, travelling generally westward but losing sight of the sun in most places.

I turned back to Jason, shouting through the cold wind that blew my voice away as soon as it escaped my mouth. "How are you holding up?"

"Fine!" he shouted back, his voice loud and strong in my ear.

"We should pull off soon," I yelled.

"Sounds good."

He could have whispered poetry to me from back there and I would have heard every word. I had to shout and risk bugs in my mouth to say anything back. I'll have to remember that, in case I ever need to tell somebody something really important. Something that they might not want to hear.

We'd only been riding for a few hours but we were already well out of the realm of familiar street signs. I'd been on this highway before, of course, but not in many years. I had no idea what lay ahead.

Eventually the road straightened, sending us due west, where the last sliver of tangerine sun was sinking into a pink grapefruit horizon. As the sun turned out the lights and climbed into bed, the road tipped Jason and me forward, and we slid down toward a lower elevation. It was warmer here, but darker too in the thickening forest. I haven't done much night riding. It wouldn't be safe on this highway with my bare knees sticking out of their shorts and Jason in a bicycle helmet.

With the loss of the sun, the gold freckles faded from the landscape and everything turned creamy blue. Those last long rays of day are always my favorite time, but the first touch of night, with the birds quieting down and the buzz of the cicadas just chiming in, is a close second.

Jason rested his chin on my shoulder; his arms still tightly clasped around my waist as if he could strap me into the world and keep me from flying up off the road and away into the stratosphere. The night breeze was cold, but Jason shared his warmth freely.

Night leaked in fast. A fancy red car skirted around us. Oaks rolled by. Still no sign of civilization.

"Do you have a map?" It was Jason, shouting into my left ear, listening in on my thoughts.

I shook my head and turned back toward him as much as I could. "No. This is an adventure."

"Life is an adventure. People still make maps."

I just shrugged. Any answer would have been lost in the wind anyway.

Venus glowed softly just above the horizon, following the sun down to bed. In another couple minutes the stars would begin to dot the sky. A green highway sign iridesced up ahead, pointing us five miles off the main road toward a town I'd never heard of, but one that promised gas, food, and lodging. I leaned into the turn and took us to a place that consisted of a McDonald's, a Shell, Bob's Auto Repair, and a motel called Motel. A painted sign proclaimed "Vacancy" with such permanence that it would have surprised me if every room were not always empty.

We pulled into the parking lot and disembarked, Jason wobbling a little when he hit the ground.

"How do we do this?" he asked.

"What do you mean?"

"How do we get a room?"

I scrunched up my nose. It hadn't occurred to me that this would be a problem. Don't you simply stride inside, slap down a shiny new credit card, and get what you point at?

"You don't exactly look eighteen. You need to be eighteen to get a hotel room."

"Credit card?" I squeaked, pulling it from my back pocket like a magic trick. Ta da.

"How did you get this?"

"I was preapproved."

"Did you activate it?"

"Did I what?"

He pulled the long red sticker from the front of the card and held it out for me on one finger. "Call this number to activate."

"Oh."

Suddenly I was a fourteen-year-old kid standing in front of a run-down motel covered in three hours' worth of dust and bugs. I was not the fearless adventurer I wanted to be.

But Jason had already dug his cell phone out of his pocket. He dialed and put the phone against my ear. After I entered an endless stream of numbers—the number on this card, your social security number, your zip code, your security code, the date you expect to die—I turned back to Jason.

"Now," I told him, breathing in my character and out myself. "Now we lie."

I blazed the trail up to the front desk.

"Excuse me," I said in my most polite child voice, throwing in an *ahem* for good measure.

"How can I help you?" And there turned around the littlest, oldest, sweetest looking lady I'd ever seen. It would have been hard to lie to her if it wasn't about to be so easy.

"The baby has been sick all day. Our dad had to take him to find a drug store, and they dropped us here and asked us to secure a room for the family. He's going to be back as soon as they get the medicine 'cause we're supposed to go visit our cousins in the morning—they live around here, and we haven't been able to see them since they came to our place last summer—but we've been driving all day, and Dad gave us the credit card that you can put the room on, and do you think it might be okay if we could give you this and get the room now?"

"Oh. Of course, sweetie. What's your name, dear?"

"Jane." I didn't skip a beat. I slid the card across the counter, slick-side down. Whoosh. That's how it begins.

"Art is your father then?"

"Yes."

"I'll just hold the card up here until he arrives."

"They might be late. I mean, I wouldn't want to keep you up or anything."

"I can hold it until the morning. How many rooms do you need? Two adjoining?"

"No, just one."

Jason perked up. "Maybe one with a sofa bed?"

"Of course. Room eight." She handed me the key, and I slipped it into my pocket. Clunk.

"Have a good night," I threw back over my shoulder. "And thank you." We walked the number line of doors until we reached eight.

"Nice work, Jane."

I unlocked the door, smirking back at him, and pushed it. It didn't budge.

"Eight, right?"

Jason pointed at the number on the door. "Yeah, eight."

"Hmm."

I pushed harder, leaning into it with all my strength. It still wasn't enough, so Jason leaned too.

"On the count of three," he said. "One, two—"

The door jolted loose and flew open wide. We tumbled straight in and would have rolled right through to the other side, but the big, puffy bed caught us safe and sound.

"Well. At least we know how to make an entrance." I sat on the edge of the bed. "Shall we see what's on TV?"

"Sure. I just need to make a phone call first."

I wished he would have left the room. I had to hear it. I had to listen to him tell his mother that his dad had come to pick him up after school. That he was sorry he didn't get a chance to say goodbye, but that he'd be home right on schedule. He'd call her from the bus stop. He loved her.

Then I had to listen to him tell his dad that he decided not to come visit. He was sorry. He'd see him this summer. He loved him.

So lying came easy for Jason, too. How very un-superhero of him.

Jason didn't ask me any questions, and I didn't ask him any, either. He sat on the bed, pointed the remote at the TV, found us an old episode of Star Trek to watch, and let me sit next to him.

I never knew that Spock used to smile so much. Reckless, illogical humans, the corners of his mouth seemed to say. That's what we were, us and James T. Kirk, moving on instinct toward some unknown future. Loving the ride just for the thrill of it.

Never looking back. Not for anything.

We fell asleep outside the covers, the Enterprise still trekking on through our dreams.

# DAY ELEVEN

It was already late in the morning by the time my eyes finally opened into thin, reluctant slits. The TV still flickered. Jason woke in the middle of the night to turn the sound down, and it was too quiet to make out what the actors said. Other than that, the room was dark. It is a necessity of motels, it seems, to do their best to fool you that the morning has not yet come. It is the nightingale and not the lark they seem to say, all the while fondling the bill with the 10 o'clock check out time. Behind the three layers of thick drapery, however, morning had all but come and gone.

Obviously our parents never returned with the baby and his medicine. I sat up and slid over to the side of the bed. Jason snoozed on unaware, content in a final pleasant dream.

He looked so young lying there. Too young to be following me in this misguided adventure. He had loving parents and good grades and a spot on the soccer team. There was plenty of time for him still; he shouldn't have to grow up so fast.

My stomach tightened and twisted around itself, as if it was a wet, dirty rag and could be clean again if it could just ring out all the grime. I shouldn't have dragged him along. I never think.

I crept from the room on heavy legs, slipping the door silently back into place, and returned to the lobby. The man behind the counter was the perfect complement to his wife. Never in a hurry, he lounged behind the counter with the sports section and a cup of coffee. It was about time for his third, I imagined, which he always told his wife was his second. She wouldn't want him drinking so much coffee every day, but that third cup was the one that really got him up and ready to get things done. *We all have our secrets,* he would say to himself to justify the little white lie that he'd been telling her for fifty years.

"Good morning, sir." I smiled sweetly and pretended to be a nice little girl.

"Good morning," he replied. His voice was surprisingly smooth, but then, coffee was his vice—not alcohol, not cigarettes. "What can I do for you?"

"I was wondering if I could get the bill for room eight and bring it over for my dad to sign. He's trying to get the baby ready to go and he's been awful fussy all morning. We're already late to see my cousins. Is it okay? If I get the bill for him? You already have the credit card."

"Room eight," the man repeated, looking up the information in his big, dusty book and swiping the card good-naturedly. I required no story to work this system, I realized. I just needed to ask for what I wanted. Less information was going to be more from here on.

He smiled at me again. "Here you go. Just bring the signed copy back with the key on your way out."

When I returned to the room, still shaking my head in mild disbelief, the shower was running. I sat down on the bed and smoothed my hair down against my head. *This is no time to take a shower*, the road screamed at me. *Get a move on*. I stared into the empty television screen and twisted my hands into the bedspread. I waited and waited and the room got warm and foggy and unbearably boring. Unable to take another second of this infinite delay, I grabbed the remote and watched a commercial break.

"Take forever!" I huffed when Jason finally stepped out of the bathroom in a cloud of steam.

He smiled and dried his hair on the towel. "Are we in a hurry or something?"

"Yes."

"Sorry. I didn't realize we had an appointment."

He wasn't moving fast enough. I rolled my eyes toward the door.

"Say," he joked, "who's our meeting with, anyway? Am I dressed for the occasion?"

"Are you ready or what?"

He shook his head but didn't drop his smile. "Just let me brush my teeth."

"There's no time for that." I flung myself onto the bed with the dramatic flair of a diva scorned. I had no patience for such nonsense as showering and brushing teeth. I had places to go.

Jason emerged again and folded up yesterday's clothes, placing them in a separate section in his backpack. "So. Where to?"

"West, Jason. Still west."

"But where west?"

"Just west." I bit my lip. "Unless you want to go home. I could take you home, you know. It's not so far."

He put his things down and sat next to me. I couldn't look at him.

"It's not too late," I offered again. "You don't need to be here."

"I'm here for you," he said simply. "Let's go."

And we were off again.

The road snaked slowly through the forest, and here, at least, the bigger cars didn't protest my lack of a need for speed. This road refused to be rushed, and something in the look of things here in the valley made that okay with me. My heart finally slowed.

We drove through the shade of the twisty, tumbling trees until we turned a corner and green became gold. There was no transition in the landscape; we just flipped to the next page and it was a different picture. The road widened and uncurled around low yellow hills dotted by oaks and only the occasional redwood. Here, the hot air stuck to the back of my throat and the highway dust began to settle over every inch of me. When the water ran off me into the tub later that night, it would look like the aftermath of a landslide.

We passed signs that pointed toward parts of the world we'd never heard of. How was public education in Smartsville? What did people eat in Timbuctoo? Did these oddly named towns, scattered a few miles off the highway, contain people just like us? Were we indistinguishable from our low-lying valley cousins?

Each turn of the road erased a few more trees from our vista until we found ourselves right in the middle of a sea of brown grass. Whenever I could, I gazed down through the rows of crops that came and went amidst the grain. I've always done it. You could put me in the back of a moving car and I would happily press my forehead to the glass, my eyes wide to soak in the repeating light/dark of planted rows and tilled earth. I could watch for lifetimes. Once, I saw fairies in the rows, silver flashes winking to me from the branches of apple trees. But it's best when there's a car or tractor moving on the other end of the field, flashing around like the pictures on a zoetrope.

Bit by bit, concrete replaced farmland until a city rose up out of the gold, long and skinny, a strip mall that stretched out for miles. Each store I passed flashed its toothy corporate grin my way, but I rode on. We'd stop for lunch in a small town, one with a story. At last the opposite side of the valley materialized out of the hazy line of smog-blue sky. I kept my eyes on the mountains up ahead until I was safely out of the paved zoo, until the fields popped back in and the trees returned, one by one.

The land began to climb again, leading us up to the shore of the state's second-biggest naturally occurring body of water. I saw its name on a brown sign and a vision of my third-grade teacher, Miss Sollars, popped into my head. That was before school had become an exercise in mediocrity; back when I was actually receiving my federally mandated education and not just drifting along.

Jason and I sat on opposite ends of a table with a view of the lake.

"So, Artemis. Inquiring minds want to know: where are we going?"

"West."

"Where are we really going?"

"I told you. I don't know. Just west."

He responded without a second's hesitation. "I don't believe you."

Jason kept his eyes locked on mine where they burned through the years of who-gives-a-fuck that I hid under. I fancied myself an all-star bullshitter, but he never let me get away with it. Truth leaked out from the fissures his gaze left behind.

"The ocean," I grumbled.

"Why?"

I scrunched my napkin into a ball beneath the table and ripped tiny pieces off it. My mouth was sticky. I reached for my water, but Jason's hand shot out and stopped me. "Because I've never been. Okay? Are you satisfied?"

He let me go. "You can't escape, you know. There's nowhere to go."

The straw from my water stuck me in the forehead. I disposed of it mercilessly.

Jason smiled and took a thoughtful bite out of his grilled vegetable panini.

Then he let it go. He nodded. "You're right. You do need to go to the beach. It's high time."

I pilfered a French fry from his plate. "Thanks," I told him.

He only smiled again and took my picture.

# NIGHT ELEVEN

We rode the motorcycle into hell. I was sure of it. I'd made a wrong turn straight into the insatiable mouth of the earth, and now we were descending at a maddening speed toward the realm of nightmares. We'd been swallowed up, rolled around behind the Devil's filthy teeth along with whirring headlights, darkness, and all the moths in the entire world. Every single last one of them.

And I'd already switched over to my reserve fuel. We would have to stop for gas.

The sun had retreated below the horizon over an hour ago. That's when the moths came, slowly at first—one splatter here, another there, hardly unusual for this time of evening. But before we knew it, we'd crossed over into some sort of hot zone, and the sticky bodies slammed into us a dozen a minute. There was no sign of an end to this attack.

I chased the signs that pointed me off toward gas/food and ever farther from the main highway. Though I pressed my lips in a tight line of defense, I could still taste the tang of dusty moth wings. Jason wasn't complaining, but then, to do so, he'd have to open his mouth and eat moths. He cringed deeper and deeper into my back, transforming my body into a Centurion's shield. This was not the adventure I had promised; it was the castigation of an angry deity, opening its mouth to hurl filth at us for some accidental transgression.

The signs lead us twelve miles from the main road before I finally found the promised gas station. The town of Gas/Food emitted a sickly yellow glow that flickered and hummed beneath the barrage of bugs. This was the kind of town that would have secreted a peculiar odor under normal, mothless circumstances. Each of these houses, lined up all alike, would smell the same inside, and folks from around these parts could tell friend from foe by nose alone.

I knew that smell was there somewhere beneath the bugs, but there was no way I could experience it this evening. My nasal cavity was clogged. I blew gobs of gray goop into a piece of binder paper I found in my pocket as Jason diligently filled the tank, cringing to half his normal height. The ends of his frown almost touched the ground.

It wasn't as bad as my overactive imagination had painted it. It was worse.

On the road, we weren't able to determine the true magnitude of the moth-plague. Here, stopped and able to look around, we could see that the swarm was of biblical proportion. It wouldn't have surprised me if it suddenly began to rain frogs or if all the firstborn children fell down dead.

Each of the gas station's lights attracted a ball of bugs that morphed and swirled with the disposition of a tropical storm. I resisted the urge to name these storms after fiery women. The orbs of insects stretched out from the lights a good six feet, each moth fighting desperately for the right to be the one that dove closest to the brightness that made them all blind and euphoric.

Along the posts and walls and ceilings and gas pumps, millions and millions of bugs crawled over each other in an effort to sober up. I don't know whether they intended to rejoin the madness of the mob or escape this city life and return to the country where honest, hardworking moths flew at the true light of the moon.

My motorcycle was yellow, but I could see no sign of its bright shoreline under the countless washed up bodies stuck to it.

Jason looked as though maybe the school bully threw him into a puddle of gray sewage. Or perhaps wet cement.

I'm sure I looked worse.

We left but had no choice other than to return the way we came, back the twelve miles of moth-covered road and through the extra thirty minutes of bug splash.

It was another hour yet before the world ran out of moths to throw at us.

We didn't speak when we got to the motel room but to explain to the wide-eyed man behind the counter that we rode a motorcycle through the fifth circle of hell.

He never even questioned my age. He just let me pay then and there, reaching the full length of his arm out whenever he needed to hand anything to me.

Jason and I dumped our clothes in the trash can and showered together in our underwear, avoiding the fight of who would clean up first.

The water ran gray for an hour as thousands of tiny wings spiraled down the drain.

# DAY TWELVE

OUR JOURNEY WEST DIDN'T END when the road did. I kept right on riding, across the Pacific Coast Highway and down the wrong way on a twisty, one-way street. I believe I might have kept riding straight into the sea if the sand a hundred yards back hadn't proven impossible to traverse. Even then, I was in such a rush that I didn't bother to turn the engine off properly; I just let it stall. I abandoned the bike behind me and continued on my straight and uninterruptable course. When my feet finally stopped at the line of sea foam, my eyes covered the rest of the distance without them—out to the far edge of the Pacific, to where the water has swallowed so much sky that it's bluer than paint.

I know that when you look up into the sky at night you're looking out across both time and space, and I know that both of these things are probably endless. But to me, it always seemed that the stars were just painted on the inside of a bowl, far above us but reachable given a long enough ladder. This was different. This felt like looking out across forever.

The air here was tangy with washed-up seaweed, a stench that would stick to the back of my throat for a long time after we left. It was ugly, too, like the dump locked up safe and sound behind its barbed wire fence. Gobs of decomposing seaweed littered the beach, attracting a billion hopping sand flies. Crab and mussel skeletons dotted the shoreline as well, and seagulls rummaged through the mess in much the same way that they explore trash of a less organic variety. They struggled noisily over any scraps they pulled from the rotting piles.

Prince should have been here to see it.

"You're supposed to take off your shoes first," Jason instructed, his already removed, and his pants rolled neatly up to his knees.

I looked down. I was standing in the water.

It was cold, as cold as the runoff from the last snow of the year which turns your skin red and makes the lake unbearable even on hot days. I turned my gaze back out to the unwavering line in the distance without responding.

No two people can see the same horizon—it's for your eyes only. Whether you're standing on the shore or a mountaintop, the horizon is always even with the exact middle of your eyes. Stretch onto tiptoe and it rises in front of you. Crouch low and it kneels to meet you. But here, at the edge of sixty-four million square miles of water, the seam between the sky and the sea rose too high in front of me. My eyes filled with ocean, and I could do nothing to shake the disconcerting feeling that these quintillions of gallons might suddenly slip loose from the distance and rush out to meet me.

Jason held a bug at me. "It's a sand crab," he said, but I was three miles away.

He put his hands back in his pockets, and we stood in the surf quietly, feeling the soft tug of the water as it foamed up along the shore. When my shoes had soaked up as much ocean as they could hold, the water started to climb into my jeans, too.

I leaned toward the sea and stepped forward.

Were I a mermaid, this would be the end of my story.

*Turning once to lift a hand of thanks, she dove below the waves and was lost beneath the foam. She had returned to her own world and no one could follow her there.*

I did dive beneath the waves, but not like that. I may be seventy percent water but there is nothing fluid about me, and the arm I lifted wasn't to wave goodbye, it was to grab a hold of something solid so I could pull myself back up for air. But there was nothing solid to steady myself on, and I toppled down to my knees. I tried to stand again but another wave slammed against my back, taking me down face first. Struggling to free myself from the water, I crawled through the surf and rolled over the tops of knee-high waves. I had seaweed in my hair and up my nose and it was a full minute before I stopped choking on the freezing, foul-smelling water.

Jason's mouth had fallen open so far his chin was at his elbows.

I spat the slimy salt out of my mouth and pulled a piece of rubbery seaweed off my head. The wind picked up and pelted me mercilessly. My body shook. I was no sea otter, but I endured the discomfort without complaint.

"What?" I said to Jason, slithering up alongside him and picking more seaweed from my clothes.

He shut his mouth and shook his head.

I had always imagined that the ocean was a stark disinfectant. I intended to arrive coated in the grime of my previous life, to dive once beneath the waves and be cleansed of the past, leaving all previous transgressions behind, like Aphrodite. Instead, the endless Pacific sucked me in and slobbered itself all over me. Beneath the salt and the cold and the seaweed and the sticky sand, I was still Artemis. Inescapably Artemis.

I dug the wet handful of papers out of my back pocket. Each had been torn from a birthday card, fourteen in all.

The torn bits were easy to conceal in one palm. I squeezed them tight, forcing the water out of them, and then turned my hand upside-down and let them tumble away. One stuck to my hand. I didn't rush it, though. I let it fall at its own pace and then turned to join Jason in the sand.

He was digging a moat.

Together, we constructed what must have been the world's biggest sand castle—truly a feat of sand engineering.

Together, we smashed it down, Jason playing Godzilla, and me The Incredible Hulk, forgetting for a moment everything we'd left behind.

When the sun had dried out my clothes and we were ready to leave, I took another long drink of the distance. Fourteen tiny "and Dads" had washed back up along the shore.

I left them where they lay.

# NIGHT TWELVE

Bang, bang, bang, bang! They didn't knock, they knocked the whole door down.

"This is the police. Get down on the floor and place your hands behind your head."

Four officers rushed into the room, guns drawn, as if I were some sort of criminal.

"Get on the floor! Now!"

I slid out of bed and did as I was told. I laid facedown and, with shaky hands, interlaced my fingers behind my head. One of the officers pointed his gun at me while the others tore the room apart.

"Where is he?" they yelled, dumping out empty drawers and digging through the extra linens on the top shelf of the closet. "What have you done with him?" They turned the bed up onto its side and cut a hole in the mattress.

"I don't know," I cried. "He was just here. I don't know where he went."

"Are you Artemis Cato?"

"Yes, yes that's me."

"You're under arrest for kidnapping. You have the right to remain silent..."

"Kidnapping? I didn't kidnap him. Jason wanted to come."

The officer stopped in the middle of his well-rehearsed speech. "Jason? Who is Jason?"

"He's my friend.

"What does he look like?"

"He has brown hair—"

The officer snarled into his radio. "Be on the lookout for a second suspect, male, brown hair."

"I didn't kidnap him. I don't understand." But he didn't care. He pressed me into the floor with his shoe and tightened a pair of handcuffs around my wrists.

"Artemis Cato, you're under arrest for the kidnapping of Prince Cato." With one of his enormous hands, he lifted me by the hair and steered me out the door toward the black and white cage.

I started to cry. "Prince isn't here. I left him with our mother. He's fine. He's at home."

"You left him behind? How long ago was that?" The car door flew open like a mouth into the backseat.

"I didn't do anything wrong. Please."

He spun me around. He had no face, just mirrored glasses, a mustache, and a thin line instead of a mouth.

"You abandoned your baby brother, left him there to rot with that slut you call a mother? Prince has been missing for four days. He's probably dead by now—those creeps don't leave them alive for long. You should have brought him with you. You never think."

As if I were nothing, the officer threw me into the car and slammed the door. I pressed my face into the plastic bench and cried so loud that I didn't hear his partner climb into the driver's seat and start the engine.

We backed out of the motel parking lot. "Hey, miss, you're going to be alright. I'm sure Prince will turn up. He's a tough boy. He can manage without you. Come on, stop crying. Things aren't that bad."

"I need a seat belt," I wailed.

"Too risky."

I sat up and kicked my feet against the barrier, hands still trapped behind my back. "It's dangerous not to wear a seat belt."

"Sorry, miss, but there are no seat belts in the backseats of police vehicles."

"You're going to kill me!" I kicked harder, right at his head, but the bars were too strong to break.

He stayed calm. "It's my job to keep you safe."

"I need Jason. What have you done with him?"

"He's fine. It's you we're worried about. We need to get you out of here."

"I don't like cops," I spat at him before wiggling into a corner to sit with my cheek on my knees. I tried my best to ignore the tingly sensation of being naked without the seat belt.

"I can see that. But you weren't safe. We had to rescue you."

"With handcuffs?"

"My job is to protect and serve, and right now I need to protect you."

"From what, exactly?"

"I wish I could explain it so that you'd understand. You just can't stay here. I have to bring you someplace safe."

"Home," I guessed. My eyes filled up with the ocean he was dragging me away from.

"No," he said, which startled me so much my tears dried up. "It's not safe there anymore."

We drove up a winding road until the hill crested down toward an orchard below. Fields of oranges filled the valley.

Near the valley floor, the cop pulled over, spoke a mouthful of coded numbers into his radio, and opened the door to let me out.

The handcuffs fell away. I rubbed on my wrists because I'd seen it done in a movie.

"Is it safe here?"

"No. I'm afraid we're too late." His eyes blurred and his shoulders rounded to the ground, heavy with failure. I'd never seen a grown man cry before, not in person, but I suspected I was about to.

"Too late for what?" The words tangled around my vocal chords. I didn't want to know. I pressed my sweaty hands to my legs because it was the only way I could keep them from jumping up against my ears to block out his response.

But it would have made no difference if I had, for the answer appeared on the horizon beyond the orange trees. There, between the mountains where it should have been only clouds and sky, was a small V of Pacific blue.

For a moment, it lingered up there, as if pausing to say hello to an old friend. Then the ocean came pouring into the valley, water covering earth until every inch of land had vanished. The flood could have easily swept us all away. We might have been a second Atlantis, millions of people drowned and discarded as myth. But the water surged in softly, without violence. It covered tractors and trees and red and white farm houses but it left them all standing. We could still live here if we would just give in and learn to breathe underwater.

I wiped off my hands. My heartbeat steadied. Even the memory of fear dissolved into nothing.

My steps light, my eyes opened, I approached the water alone. With nothing to protect me from, the cop dissolved in my wake.

Remembering what Jason told me at the beach, I removed my shoes and left them behind on the side of the road. Unhindered at last, I stepped into the sea.

It was warm, so I dove in.

The smooth water enveloped me like a first love. It touched me everywhere and held me up so that I could float on its surface effortlessly. I rolled and splashed and swam to the top of a tree that poked up like an island. Up in the branches, I dangled my feet in the water and pulled apart liquid sections of orange.

It would have been pointless to try and stop this flood, but I could just imagine thousands of people with their sandbags all lined up anyway, a ridiculous barrier against the inevitable. We were impotent in the face of nature—inconsequential as sugar ants.

Only our egos told us otherwise.

I smiled; the orange peel in my mouth a tribute to the setting sun. It was the most I could do.

# DAY THIRTEEN

Beads of sweat welled up from the pores in my forehead and tumbled down to the starchy white sheets. Jason shook my shoulder back and forth, jostling me back into the waking world.

Struggling to free myself, I sat up and kicked the sweltering blankets away.

"What's the matter?" Jason asked, his voice still scratchy from sleep.

I shook my head and reached for my water bottle. There was nothing wrong.

"Did you have a bad dream?"

I didn't want him to know so I shook my head again. "Why did you wake me up?"

"You were talking. You sounded upset."

"I was talking?" The shock of being forced from my dreams melted away beneath the shock of this revelation. "What did I say?"

"Nothing really. You were just mumbling like usual. But this time it sounded like you were struggling, like you were upset. It wasn't coherent."

"You mean I've done this before?"

"Yes."

"Why didn't you tell me?"

"How was I supposed to know you didn't know?"

"How would I know? I was asleep?"

"Hey, calm down. It's okay. The things you say don't make any sense. I wouldn't worry about it. I mean, it scared me a little the first time but then it was kind of funny, what you were saying."

"What was I saying?"

"You said, 'Pop it popcorn! Pop pop pop!' Just like that."

I laughed a little at his reenactment of the pops. "I don't like popcorn."

"Yeah, dreams don't usually make any sense." He took his hand from my shoulder and his face darkened. "But if I were you, I'd be careful who you tell that you don't like popcorn. You could get arrested. It's un-American."

"Please don't report me."

He sucked a long breath in through his teeth. "No promises."

I smiled at him and caught sight of the clock out of the corner of my eye: 6:37. May as well get started early.

☼ ☼ ☼

OUT OF WEST, WE TURNED the bike ninety degrees to the right and wound our way up the Coastal Range. There was no sky here, just sweet-smelling earth and trees that stretched up to the stars. From time to time, the Pacific would peek in on us, just to make sure we were still okay. When she saw that we were, she would smile and close the curtain of rust-red trees around us again.

This was the most peaceful forest I'd ever been in. For a while, I was able to follow the curves of the road and forget to worry. But my sense of Zen was short lived.

A police car turned onto the highway behind us.

"Stay cool," I told Jason.

"What?" he asked, but I didn't repeat myself.

I kept my eyes locked on the black and white cruiser in the mirror. Cops make me so self-conscious that I drive like I'm stupid. I was going to make a dumb mistake. He was going to pull us over. I just knew it. He tailed me for five minutes, then, sure enough, turned on his lights.

"Oh, fuck!" I squealed. My arms were shaking, my mouth had run dry, and Jason was twisting the sides of my shirt into his fists.

"What do we do?"

"Shit."

I signaled and slowly pulled onto the shoulder. But he didn't stop; he sped up, passed us, and turned off his flashers.

I came to a complete stop and watched him drive away. "What a jerk."

"He really wanted you to get out of his way."

"I can't believe it."

"You drive way too slow, Artemis. People got plans. People got places to be. They can't be waiting on you."

Jason laughed at his joke and, after a minute, I did too.

The panic subsiding, I took a moment to look around.

"Hey. What is that?" I pointed at one of the trees up ahead. It had what appeared to be a hot-pink flamingo nailed to it.

"It's a flamingo. You haven't noticed them?"

"No."

"We passed dozens."

"I was driving."

"Oh."

I walked up to it. Yes, that was a large, foam flamingo nailed through the head into a tree. "What do you think it's for?"

"I'm not sure. Maybe they're there to mark the trees that have nests?"

"Of what? Greater Redwood Flamingo?"

Jason shrugged. "Maybe."

"Yeah, I don't think that's a thing."

"No, that's totally a thing," he said. "Didn't you study Native Americans in third grade?"

I turned to him. "What?"

"Didn't you?"

"Yes."

"Yeah, then you know. You read the story of how Coyote stole Flamingo's feathers and used them to win the all-animal costume contest."

"You're ridiculous."

"No, it's true. Flamingo was so ashamed to arrive at the contest naked that he blushed bright pink and hid his head under his wing so the other animals wouldn't see his face."

"Let's go."

"And he's still doing it to this very day."

"Come on."

It was still early when we arrived in town. I parked the bike in front of a coffee shop.

This place had a familiar smell. I'd noticed it from the road but I couldn't quite place it. Maybe the fishbowl, when we returned from Grandma's to find Goldie dead. My mother made me fish her out from under the castle with a spoon, a task that took me an hour because I didn't want to touch the water. I carried her to the toilet, trying not to cry or throw up. Or perhaps the smell was more like my copy of *The Hobbit,* which had been left out in the rain overnight. I refused to replace it. Instead, I blew it out page by page with the hair dryer. I knew the smell of that book well because I kept it by my bed for three months, doling out the pages only a few at a time before it finally disappeared one day. I hope things worked out for Bilbo. I never did find out.

We entered the building where the coffee smell masked the peculiar odor of the town to all but the most astute of observers.

Behind the counter hung a calendar with a picture of a kitten and a big black X through every day that had already been. Today, I noticed, had been crossed out. Life was just one big countdown to death.

I'm fairly sure I was frowning when I ordered my drink from the pale girl in the burial shroud. Gloom hovered above her like her own personal rain cloud. I felt rotten until I was given a miniature spoon to stir my cappuccino with. Then I sat down on a dishwater-green couch and scooped tiny mouthfuls of foam from my drink, pretending I was twenty feet tall.

"The objects here in the land of humans are merely tiny toys, terribly breakable in my enormous hands."

Jason shook his head. "You're so weird."

I considered requesting an espresso cup, just to be able to play Enormous a little better, but Elvira shot a death stare at me so I sat back down.

She scowled at each customer in turn, preparing their drinks with an elaborate show of disdain. Her black bangs and black tee shirt and black spiky bracelets had seeped into her bloodstream and killed off all her joy. How can a person feel alive if they're starving for color?

"I hope her sister died or something," I said out loud from the depths of the couch.

"What?" Jason locked eyes with me and placed a hand on my knee, a warning to choose my next words very carefully.

"I mean—I didn't mean it like that. What I meant was that I hope the reason she's so sordid and dark is that something bad happened recently. I mean—I hope she isn't always so unhappy. I hope she smiles sometimes."

Jason released my knee and looked over to her. She leaned against the kitten calendar, her arms crossed tight around herself, completely miserable. "Hmm... Yeah, I see what you're saying. But do me a favor. Don't say that kind of thing to regular people."

"What's Regular People?"

"The kind who don't know you well. The kind who won't bother taking the time to understand you. The kind who don't lo— Who don't care about you." His lips and cheeks flushed and he had to look away.

A wooziness rushed through my veins. A double was too much caffeine.

Jason and I settled silently into the couch, which held us like a nervous mother—close and uncomfortably deep.

There was something in that moment that surpassed my expectations of Jason Messenger.

"I'm glad you're here," I whispered.

# NIGHT THIRTEEN

Her hair fanned out like water behind her as she glided away down the stairs.

I reached for her sleeve to stop her. "Mom," I yelled, but there was nothing solid for me to grasp. Her paper-thin gown slipped through my fingers. "Mom!" I grabbed for her again and missed. By the time I called for her a third time, she was out of earshot. She moved so fast.

I had no choice but to follow, to force myself down the stairs after her. Above me, the flickering florescent lights rattled like angry wasps, warning me to stay back. This was not my territory. I was out of my depth.

"I have to get her back," I told them.

They kept on rattling.

As I flew from one floor to the next, I caught the occasional glimpse of her, winding her way down at a reckless pace. I couldn't catch up. I couldn't stop her.

"Mom! Mom! Don't leave me."

She wouldn't turn.

Tears spilled out of my eyes in a sudden downpour; my body rumbled with thunder.

Just when I thought I'd never catch up, I reached the bottom step and found myself in front of a hallway of opened doors that stretched out endlessly. They opened away from me so I couldn't see what was inside.

I stepped into the hall, reaching for the nearest door, but no sooner had I brushed my fingers against the wood than it pulled away and slammed shut. The sound was so sharp and final that I jumped, my tears pouring out again in two steady streams.

"Mom? Open your door. I had a bad dream. Please, open the door."

I lacked the strength to pry it away from its frame so, shaking, I moved to the next one.

Once again, the moment my hands reached it, it drew away and threw itself closed.

Sobbing loudly and meandering down the hall of slamming doors, I continued the futile search for my mother. I was only instinct walking.

SLAM! SLAM! SLAM!

Screaming now, I reached for a closed door and pulled with every ounce of strength I had. But it held fast.

"Mom! Mom! Open your door."

I yanked until I was sure I was going to rip my arms from their sockets, and then I sunk to the floor, tears gushing from my eyes, fingernails scratching holes in my skin, crying for my mom.

The wind appeared like a whisper and grew into a gale I could not resist. It pushed me out of the hall, leaving all the doors opened again in its wake. It pushed me up the stairs and out of the stairwell. It pushed me all the way back up to my bed where I woke still sobbing.

Jason slept quietly beside me. I wondered if I had spoken during that dream. If I had, it hadn't disturbed him.

I waited for the piercing claws of fear to loosen and then slipped quietly out of the bed. I had to make a phone call. I floated to the other side of the room like a ghost.

When I opened the door, it creaked as if it were trying to wake Jason. My eyes swept over to him automatically, but it was too dark to see. I opened the door another couple inches, just wide enough to squeeze through and found myself in the red and orange hallway.

Barefoot, I padded softly to the elevator and journeyed quickly down the four stories, keeping my back pressed against the corner.

A few people still milled about the lobby, all staff as far as I could tell. It was 2:15.

I approached a bored bellman and asked for a phone. He pointed without looking up from texting.

The familiar numbers flew out of my fingers.

What would I say to her when she picked up? How would I explain? Would I ask her if things were okay or would I demand an explanation for everything she'd done?

Ring, ring, ring.

She should have picked up by now. Prince would get to the phone before she did.

Ring, ring, ring.

I listened to the phone ring for ten minutes before I finally gave up and returned to bed.

But I didn't sleep again that night.

# DAY FOURTEEN

I DIDN'T WANT TO TALK about it. I just needed to keep it locked up in my head. It wouldn't have to be real if I didn't let it out.

At 6:21, Jason rolled onto his side.

"Are you awake," I asked in his ear.

He was now.

"Fantastic. Let's get another early start. Come on, let's get going." I practically rolled him off the bed and into the bathroom so he could shower. I don't even think his eyes were open yet.

Being on the road didn't make me feel better though. Every bump rose up an extra sixteen inches, amplified by fatigue and worry. But no matter how the bike jostled me, it couldn't shake the crickets out of my stomach. I kept fantasizing that I would pull into the driveway to see something horrible: the burned out remains of the house, Police Line: Do Not Cross tape, my mother and father and Prince sitting around the dinner table pretending not to know me. Every time the panic subsided, guilt rose up to take its place.

I felt sick. Sick, sick, sick. And heavy, too. I'm surprised I didn't pop the tires.

Jason must have known something was up. He rested his chin on my shoulder, but all it did was dig out a sore spot.

My mind refused to shut up.

What did it mean anyway? So no one answered the phone? So what? They could have slept through my call. The receiver could have run out of battery. My father could have come back again and taken the phone with him. Anything. So it kept ringing. So what? It didn't mean anything.

I guess it meant we'd paid the phone bill.

We crossed the state line. Local cops would have to turn around here, but there were none on our tail.

But what if it did mean something?

*Shut up*, I told myself.

Jason hugged me harder.

Finally, just when I was about to drive myself completely crazy, the rain found us. Considering the time of year, we'd been lucky with the weather. Today, our luck tipped over and poured out onto us. I didn't mind. It was so cold it made my brain and heart numb. I could have ridden all day, stiff and soggy in the freezing downpour, but Jason shivered against me so I pulled into the next town I saw.

If there was something remarkable about this place it was the color. It was like riding into a black and white movie. I didn't even know there were so many shades of gray to choose from. The sky was gray and the sea was gray and the tideland was gray and the peeling paint on the houses was gray. The rain even washed away all of Jason's colors, leaving him gray, too. But there was no question of which gray was which. After all, grayscale or not, Lucy is still a redhead.

Sopping wet, we slunk into the hotel like the pair of transient children we were. It was here, of all places, that we were first turned away. We'd gotten so used to the world's disregard that we'd stopped playing the con.

"Where are your parents?" The suspicious gray man asked.

"Uh," was all I could think to respond.

Unfortunately, Jason jumped in. "They had to take the baby to get medicine and they sent us up ahead to get the room for when they get back so we can visit our cousins tomorrow." The rain, it seemed, had numbed his brain a little, too.

"What?"

Jason nudged me for help, but I could see the job was already botched so I shook my head and tried to pull him back out the door.

He didn't budge. "Our dad took the baby and went to get her some medicine. Can we check in for him and go change out of our wet clothes?"

"How did you get so wet?"

"From the motorcycle."

"Your dad takes the two of you and a baby on a motorcycle on a family trip?"

"Gotcha!" I yelled and grabbed Jason by the sleeve—I practically threw him on the bike—revved up and was out of there before the clerk had time to come out from behind the counter.

This was no time to screw up a whole town full of motels. At the next place, we took a moment to work out a plan before we walked in, but the woman behind the counter was busy arguing on the phone so she let us sign for the room with a dismissive wave of her hand.

We stumbled inside, ordered a pizza, and used up every last drop of hot water in the county before settling in for an early night.

# NIGHT FOURTEEN

We were only a day away now. The road led me steadily north and, though I hadn't yet revealed my destination to Jason, there was purpose to my wandering. Tomorrow we would be there, and the thought of seeing her again made my stomach do little flips around the pepperoni and the pineapples. It's strange that we say we feel with our hearts when the physical center of our emotion is so obviously a few inches lower.

Jason always seemed to know where to look to find Star Trek. My interest in the phenomenon had so far been limited to the fact that Kirk and Spock are pretty much delicious in the new movies. I have to admit, though, I am enjoying the journey through these old episodes. The Starfleet pants come up too high and don't end low enough and the effects are ridiculous, but I can see how it was groundbreaking.

I watched upside-down, with my head in the center of the bed and my feet resting against the headboard. Jason lounged on the bed in the regular way, his hands behind his head. If I turned my nose to the right, his nose would be only a few inches from mine.

And I did.

And he did.

And the last thing I heard from the TV was, "Phasers on stun," before I forgot who I was in a single kiss. His mouth was softer than I thought it would be, and there was none of that garbled Hollywood movie game of whose tongue is whose. It was clean and simple, and I could tell him from me because he was on one side of the kiss and I was on the other. We held onto that moment. Neither of us moved to break away or to close the last molecule of distance.

There was something alien about Jason. He smelled like a boy. Not sweaty and pungent like a man who works with tools in the sun, but brave and strong just the same. He didn't smell like a movie star, but there was something I couldn't quite identify that I needed more of, an addictive intoxicant in the scent of his skin and in the sting of something spicy that lingered on his lips.

I tried to measure the event, to memorize the details of who started it and how long it lasted, but all possible answers seemed equally as likely. It refused to be defined. It was simply the next step. We took it as logically as our next breath of air. I kissed Jason Messenger because I was supposed to.

My life was a river that flowed down a path traced in stone, and I couldn't dam it up or change its course. Like water running downhill, my lips flooded into Jason's.

When I came up from the dark quiet of that moment, I left a part of myself behind. Things could no longer be the same.

I opened my eyes and pulled my head back to let Jason come into focus. There was nothing in his eyes to betray what the kiss had done to him. He watched me patiently in the flickering light of the TV.

My face burned. My lips melted away. My body screamed and twisted and tightened in on itself though I remained perfectly still. This wasn't right. It was supposed to happen, but it wasn't right.

With a steady hand Jason cleared away a tear that hadn't yet slid down my cheek.

"Got room on that credit card of yours for a movie rental?" he asked me easily.

I nodded, sniffled into my palm, and slid my body back around the right way, my chin planted clumsily on the knees I clasped between my sweaty palms.

"I think an action movie. Maybe one based on a comic book."

I nodded. My heart pounded against my ribs, fighting for a freedom I could not allow it.

Jason searched the TV menu for just the right Pay-Per-View film. He was unfazed by what had transpired between us; for him, everything was the same.

I hugged my knees tighter and fought against the ocean of tears that threatened the corners of my eyes.

Jason scooted next to me, leaned back against the headboard, and reached up a hand that looked like it was headed for mine.

How could I brush it away? How could I head us back toward safety?

He flicked a piece of dust off the covers between us and returned his hand to his own lap.

I allowed the film to distract me and Jason to sit there on the other side of the chasm that ran between us.

If it had been as deep and as wide as the Grand Canyon, I could still have filled it with the tears I now held back.

And I have no doubt that all I had to do was ask, and Jason would swim across it to me, current be damned.

# DAY FIFTEEN

I WOKE UP EARLY WITH my cheek on Jason's shoulder. The creases in his shirt had etched lines across my face that felt like scars when I ran my fingers over them.

We left in a hurry while the air was still cold and the light was still gray and wispy through the fog. I turned us to the northeast, away from the sea, toward a past that I remembered well.

I hadn't told Jason where we were going, but in a few more hours that wouldn't matter. We'd unlock the gate to the backyard, and she'd scoop us up into her arms, and everything would be made clear. She'd know what to do next.

With the ocean behind us, the grays and blues fell away. A pallet of greens replaced them: apple, asparagus, lime, olive, spring, shamrock, jungle, hunter, mint, mantis, India. The verdant landscape was broken only by the occasional patches of orange and red and purple spring flowers.

We rode past breakfast and lunch, and the vibration of the road lulled us into a complacent emptiness. I was less the body of a girl and more a temporary collection of thought and breeze. Jason followed me like my shadow, silently pulled along by two fiercely spinning wheels and my will to arrive.

At a small, unremarkable town, I veered away from the highway and drove through a series of familiar streets. I still had the place memorized despite the years I had been away.

We parked the motorcycle and tip-toed up to the quiet house. On the porch, we were greeted by a box of unopened mail and rolled-up newspapers. I placed my hand on the doorknob but thought better of it and knocked.

No one answered, but the box of mail could have told me that.

"Are you looking for Mrs. Laurent?"

I didn't look up to see who was asking. I had my hand on the doorknob, trying to turn it back and forth, impeded by the lock.

"Yes," Jason answered.

"You the Murphy kids?"

"Yes," he said again.

"She's still in Singapore."

"Oh."

Laying my cheek against the cold glass of the window, I peeked inside.

"She's due back in a week or so. I'm sure she'll give you a call then."

"Oh. Okay."

It was dim in the house, but as clean and well-kept as ever.

"You kids mow lawns, too, or just pull weeds?"

"No."

The couch was covered in a horrid pink floral from some other century, and an assortment of cooking and gardening magazines were fanned out across the coffee table. Nearby, an iron lamp balanced precariously on its three uneven legs.

"You sure? I'll pay you twenty bucks."

"No, thanks. I think we'll just leave her a note to call us."

"Okay. Have a good day, kids."

If I closed my eyes, I could feel the soft cushions beneath me as I curled up under the lamp, flipping through pages of cakes and dinner party spreads and fancy drinks.

"Sorry," Jason whispered, but I shook my head.

The kitchen would be humming to life in the background. Prince would be napping in his crib, but we would wake him when dinner was ready and move the entire party out to the patio table to eat amongst the butterfly bushes and jacaranda trees.

Prince wouldn't be napping in his crib, though. He had grown up since then. The years had wrapped themselves around him, one on top of the other, hiding the soft heart of him from the world. He wasn't a baby anymore. Opening my eyes, I slid back from the glass, my face cold. I slipped around the side of the house and reached my hand up over the fence to free the lock. It wasn't going to be all for nothing. I took two slow breaths and pictured it perfectly in my mind. The swing, the trees, the fountain, the flowers, the stone steps up to the house. Then, I let go of the gate and crossed over into Wonderland.

It was smaller than it used to be.

Green plants dotted the dark earth like small islands in the yard. But the vines weren't as sprawling, the butterflies weren't as abundant, and the jacaranda wasn't as purple as it had been before I opened the gate. It was just a garden. A nice, simple garden. I drifted inside still holding onto one last shred of hope that the mundane could be miraculously transformed. But this was no mystical world. The ordinary wooden gate was not a portal into a dream. It didn't lead me anywhere but into my grandmother's backyard.

"We can go," I whispered, my voice so soft that the slightest breeze blew it far out of reach.

Jason stood quietly beside me, smiling into the clumps of irises and empty patches of dirt. "This is remarkable."

I watched him through liquid eyes. He breathed the green in all the way down to his toes. "It's not," I informed him. "It's a garden. Nothing more."

"But it is."

"No, Jason, it's not. I thought that it was something special, but I was wrong. It's just a garden."

He sighed, turning his camera over in his hands.

"I'll show you," he said, but he wasn't going to be able to take a picture of something that simply wasn't there. He couldn't find what I'd lost.

I sat on the porch swing, one leg tucked under my body, the other pushing me back and forth, while Jason moved through the yard and took pictures of dirt, bugs, and leaves.

"You spend so much time looking for what's wrong with everything," he said at last, sitting down next to me, "that you've forgotten how much right there still is in the world."

I scooted away from him and ran my fingers across the tops of the unopened tulips.

"Why are we here?"

I shook my head.

"I'm sorry your grandmother's gone."

The tulips danced back and forth in the breeze.

"I'm glad I got to see her garden, though. Now I know where Prince gets it from. It really is special."

Soft tears trickled slowly from my eyes. "It's not," I said. "It's not special." I slid off the swing and knelt in the dirt.

He sat down beside me. "It's a part of you. It's a part of you I've never been able to see until now. That makes this place very special. To you and to me."

I reached for the garden, trying desperately to hold onto something, but the soil came loose in my hands. I lowered my head and sobbed into the leaves and the roots.

"Look up."

I shook my head.

"Look up. The light."

When I did, Jason snapped my picture.

"I'm a mess! Delete that!"

He looked at the view screen and shook his head. "I wish you could see what I see."

I snatched the camera from his hands and almost threw it in the fountain—but then I saw the picture. My face was a disaster, smudged over with tears and dirt. My hair was a train wreck after the hours compressed in a helmet. My clothes were ragged from the road and the soil in the garden.

But the light was perfect.

Somehow the light was just perfect.

Jason lifted me up and carried me from the garden. On the bike, hidden from the wind for the first time, I spilled tears down the back of his neck. I leaned my face against his shoulder and let my mind rest. He drove us south until it was sunset and then selected a nondescript motel beside a nondescript Chinese restaurant.

In the motel room, I showered while Jason watched an ocean documentary. I turned the water as hot as it would go and let it sear the years from my skin. My face was caked in a layer of salt thicker than the Pacific had left on me. But it rinsed clean without protest. I'd hoped it wouldn't have come off so easily—I'd wanted to have to peel away the layers, to pry off every last hope, every last illusion. But they all came away at once, leaving me suddenly naked in the rushing water. Even the knots pressed into my hair by the wind and the helmet slipped loose after the first dose of conditioner. I lingered in the hot water with nothing to do; breathing the steam and watching my skin turn pink. I waited there until the heat made me dizzy.

When at last I emerged, we walked to the Chinese place and split orders of chow mein and cashew chicken. I took Jason's camera and flipped through the pictures.

"You have a wonderful eye for composition," I told him quietly.

"What do you mean?"

"I don't know. That's just what my art teacher says sometimes in class. Not to me; I just hear it."

He smiled. "I take pictures of things I find beautiful."

"I don't look beautiful in this." I showed him the picture he took to prove it.

"No. Not in a classical sense. But this picture is honest, and I think there's a great deal of beauty in honesty. I found your grandmother's garden honest, too. I think I would know her just from having seen it."

"It wasn't what I hoped it was going to be."

"I know."

"It didn't make things make sense."

"Maybe things don't."

I paused and then forced myself to ask. "Why did you come with me?"

"I worry about you," he answered without hesitation. "Sometimes I think you're headed at full speed toward self-annihilation."

"What if I'm too far gone?"

"You're not. You just need to be more careful with yourself. I know that everything's not okay, and I wish you would tell me why, but I get it. I know that it's too hard to say these things. And I know that sometimes you have to break something apart before you can put it back together right. It's not easy, either. If you break it down too much you won't be able to fix it, and if you don't break it enough, it's all for nothing. It's hard to find that balance, and I don't think anyone should have to do it alone. Someone has to be there to keep an eye on all the loose pieces."

I smiled dimly, but the broken pieces of me started to slip out of place, like Prince's LEGOs tumbling over themselves in their rush to escape.

Like rats jumping off a sinking ship.

# NIGHT FIFTEEN

I HATE THE DARK. I always have. Turn out the lights, and I transform into a creature that's made of claws and panic. Once when I was five, my mother, furious with me for something I can't remember, threw me into my room and held the door shut as I screamed and wailed and tried to scratch a hole through the floor to escape. Eventually, I curled up into a ball next to the door and hid there for hours. I hated her for days after that; not because I was angry or right but because she left me there in the dark and she should have known that I was too afraid to walk across the room to turn on the light.

And it wasn't even that dark in my room.

In the cave, the darkness was complete. I wrapped my arms around my legs, pressed my head down onto my knees, and squeezed my eyes shut. I didn't want to have to move. I would rather have died, collapsed in on myself like an expired star, than walk across the room to turn on the light, because I didn't know if there was even a light there.

But something inside whispered to me urgently. "Move," it said, and I did.

Blind, I pressed my hands out to the sides. There wasn't much space. My elbows crowded into my ribcage, the top of my head brushed the fiercely cold ceiling and my knees ground into the slick stone floor. I was entombed in this solid world of utter darkness, stuck in an Artemis-sized pit. Nothing existed but the stone all around me and the distant echo of a single drop of water sliding forever into a lightless pond.

I was too terrified to scream. I sat frozen, a statue in the void, pressing my hands into the walls as hard as I could because if I didn't press the walls away they might squeeze in closer. I had to force myself to suck up each mouthful of air, gulping at it the way a fish does, in large pointless gasps.

"It's only a dream, it's only a dream," I mumbled over and over but it didn't help. If I couldn't escape this place, I was going to die here, dream or not.

Drip. Drip. Drip.

Slow and regular—like Jason's heartbeat in the morning before he opened his eyes—as he brushed careless fingertips along my arm.

Drip. Drip. Drip.

I let the sound into my body, gave it control of me. I forced my heart to beat along in time, and made my breath keep this even rhythm.

Drip. Drip. Drip. Beat. Beat. Breathe.

The water trickled down and fell into a pool some distance away from me.

Wait. If I were stuck behind solid stone, I wouldn't have been able to hear it. This wasn't a tomb, it was a tunnel. Sure enough, there was empty space in front of me.

I brought my hands to the floor and slid my fingers across the smooth surface, reaching out and out and out. I scooted my knees up to meet them. Again. Slide out, out, out, shuffle forward.

At first, my movement was limited to this painfully slow, inadequate inching forward but, after a distance with no obstacles and no registerable change in the tunnel, I gained the confidence to crawl on one hand and both knees. My second hand I kept in front of me in search of the end of the corridor.

I followed the sound of the water until a drop of it landed on my nose and rolled down my lips, leaving its chalky kiss behind. The pool was only a puddle that slanted downhill in a long, slimy decline. I followed the trail of water down until there was room enough to stand but walking turned out to be a dangerous means of locomotion in this underworld. I only tried it for a few steps before I slammed my knee into a misplaced stalagmite. The pain was alarming. I pressed my fingers against the spot, feeling the soft swell of a bruise already forming—as if this all were real.

After a ways, the rock beneath my fingers dried out and a dingy brown light refracted off the quartz-studded granite. I moved toward it, following the curve in the cave up and out into an open room where I could finally see well enough to stand again. I kept my arms out for balance and limped along until the cave finally spat me out into the sunlight.

It was no relief. I had wished for day to break over my dreamscape, but this sun was far more oppressive than the night I had just endured.

Squinting against the glare, I did my best to take in my new surroundings. The desert stretched out endlessly in all directions, but the bright white light reflecting off it kept me from taking in too much at once. I blinked away streaming, sun-filled tears.

My knee cried out when I shifted my weight onto it. Sure enough, it had turned dark purple and the skin across the top was torn and bloody. A smear of red leaked down my shin. I poked at my injured knee. It retaliated, shooting a wave of sticky-sweet pain so strong I could feel it all the way to the bridge of my nose. But I did not favor it as I stepped out into the blinding light to stumble across the metallic desert.

When my eyes finally gave up their mutiny and stopped squeezing back shut the moment I opened them, I noticed a blue figure off in the distance. He turned his face to me, his eyes two black disks. There was nowhere else to go, so I stumbled toward him on loose stones that forbade even the idea of a plant.

I walked for what seemed to be hours. My skin grew wet with the exertion. By the time I reached the figure who was not blue himself but only dressed in blue, he had turned his back to me.

I put my hand on his shoulder and spun him around.

It was Jason.

The details were so clear. I could see the flecks of gold and green in his eyes, the pores on the tip of his nose, and each of the fibers in the blue cloth that covered him. I might have been looking at him under a microscope. A stray thread attempted to escape from a small tear. I watched that tear for a long time.

"You're so real," I said at last.

"I am," he agreed.

"But how?"

"Simple. I am real. You are the dream."

I felt myself starting to fall, tilting like a slowing top.

"Wake up and it's over," he went on. "All of it."

"That's not right."

"Wake up!"

He shoved me. The shock of his touch sent me zooming back to the motel where I awoke drenched and shaking.

# DAY SIXTEEN

I CARRIED AN INFLATABLE TURTLE in one hand and a shark in the other. I would have carried them all the way to the check-out counter, but Jason stopped me.

"What's this?" he asked.

He'd been hard at work picking out a tent, examining each of the miniatures propped up along the aisle.

"You said we needed pool floats to sleep on. I got us pool floats."

Jason laughed. "You're going to sleep on a shark?"

"Actually, I thought I'd take the turtle. That fin doesn't look too comfortable."

"I'm not taking you camping if you won't get the right gear."

"No one asked you to take me camping." I tried to say it teasing, but it came out full of spikes.

"No one asked you to take me to the beach," he snarked back, crossing his arms.

I bit my lip. I didn't want to fight with him, even if it was only play. "Not true. Ringo told me to bring you to the beach."

"Ringo?"

"Yeah. The bike. How do you not know this?"

Jason smiled and, with a hand on each of my shoulders, pushed me out of the camping aisle and into the store at large. "Regular pool floats!"

I saluted. "Yes sir, Mr. Super-Serious-Camping-Guy."

"That's right. Camping is serious business. Don't you forget it."

We packed the gear in the sidecar and worked our way up to a higher elevation where the air was noticeably cooler, even in the warmth of the mid-afternoon sun. I let him tell me where to go. To be honest, it was kind of a relief not to have to decide things, like coming up from the bottom of the pool after holding your breath just as long as you possibly could.

Jason, it turns out, is an expert at tent construction. Our shelter was ready to go five minutes after we picked out our site, the one with the level picnic table and chair-shaped sitting rock. I'd hopped off the bike, paused for a moment to admire the pine trees, and then turned around to find Jason anchoring the rain fly. He was like some sort of camp wizard. I told him so.

"No, I'm just me. Just the same old regular Super-Serious-Camping-Guy you've known all along. Now, blow up the mattresses so I can build us a fire. It's freezing up here."

The tent was roomy, tall enough to stand up in and wide enough to maintain the illusion that we were here only as friends. I sat inside with my shoes hanging out the front and huffed and puffed into the two regular pool floats until my brain somersaulted around so much that little swirly white stars danced around my eyes. I paused, the pink plastic mattress still limp in my hands. No matter how much thin air I sucked in, I couldn't catch my breath.

"Are you okay?" Jason asked, crawling into the tent.

My head rested against something hard, and it took me a minute to realize that I was lying down. "Uh... yeah," I stammered, rising up and leaning too far forward, dizzying myself once more. "It's just hard to breathe in all this fresh air and nature, I guess."

"Yeah. Pace yourself with those mattresses, okay?" He smiled and went back to his collection of sticks and pine needles.

I smiled back and returned the valve to my mouth, this time taking slower, more measured breaths.

When I had decorated the interior of the tent to my satisfaction (and after a brief rest to try out the new beds), I emerged from our canvas home, zipped the front door closed, and went to see how Jason was doing with the fire. He had meticulously arranged his sticks into a pile that looked just like a pile of sticks. I sat on my rock chair and watched him light a handful of pine needles and blow them out.

"Aren't you doing that wrong?"

He looked up at me, still blowing on what used to be a fire. "Have you ever made a fire?"

I shook my head. "Nope."

"You have to blow on it to get it started."

"You blow a fire out. Like the candles on a birthday cake. You blow them *out* so the cake doesn't catch the house on fire. You don't blow them on."

He laughed and continued puffing onto the sticks.

"No seriously, Jason—"

But I was cut short by a sudden burst of orange that crept up from under one small log and crackled to life beneath it. The needles shriveled away and a red-orange tongue of flame began to lick at the bark.

We wrapped potatoes in foil and placed them in the fire.

The sunlight faded slowly, taking its time and leaving us with long hours of twilight. The air chilled even more, and soon we were wrapped in open sleeping bags, the plastic on the soles of our shoes softening in the fire.

"Artemis?" Jason asked after checking on the still-raw potatoes again. "Do you think your parents are worried about you?"

I hadn't told him about the call. I hadn't told him that it was me who was worried about *them.*

I closed my eyes tight and answered softly. "No."

"I bet you're wrong."

I nodded but insisted. "My father's gone and my mother's drunk. Odds are no one's even noticed my absence."

Leaving his hands in his lap, Jason leaned his shoulder into mine. "What about Prince?"

"What about him?"

"I bet he misses you. I bet he knows you're gone."

"He hates me."

"Come on. He's six. He doesn't really hate you. When I was six, I told Hayley Anderson that I hated her after she stepped in a puddle and splashed mud on my brand new Batman shoes. 'I hate you, Hayley Anderson,' I said, and I'm pretty sure I didn't tell her why. She shoved me into a pile of gravel the next day and a week later I asked her for the green marker and she let me use it. We never talked about it, but I think that marked the end of the feud."

"Oh no. I told her to push you." I hid my face behind my hand, but I'm sure he could see that I was smiling underneath it.

He laughed. "You did?"

"Yeah. I did. I hadn't remembered that until just now."

"Artemis, that's so mean. How could you?"

I shook my head and sunk my forehead to my knees. I was laughing too hard to answer.

"If I'd have known it was you all along... Well. I don't know how I could have been friends with you all these years. Oh, well. I guess it's too late now. But if I had a time machine, I'd go back and unfriend you so fast." He nudged me. "Anyway, the point is that six-year-olds get mad and don't know what to do with it. He doesn't hate you. He's hurt. And that's not your fault. Once he figures that out you two will be fine."

"I'm just so tired of having to be the adult all the time. I can't take care of him. I can't even take care of me. I don't know what to do."

Jason frowned at the fire and rolled our potatoes over with a long stick.

"How about your parents? Do you think they've figured out that you've escaped into the wild?" I asked when the silence became too thick with the crackle of the flames and the approaching darkness.

"No. They won't check in with each other."

"Really?"

"They don't speak to each other anymore. Ever. When I was eight, they started using me as their courier, and then, a few years later, they only spoke through their lawyers. Now, in the rare instances when they need to communicate it goes through me again. It's easier that way. There's a lot less yelling in my life."

"What happened?"

He shook his head. "I don't know. Things fell apart. Does it matter why?"

I poked the fire with my poking stick, releasing tiny baby fires into the sky. Their freedom was always short-lived. "No. I guess not."

"But things do get better. I promise."

"Even the really sucky things?"

"Yeah. Especially those."

I smiled and nudged Jason back. For the first time in my life, I had company.

"Crazy Eights?" Jason pulled a deck of cards out from his pocket.

I didn't tell him I thought Crazy Eights was a lame card game.

After two hours and twenty minutes, we rolled the world's longest-baked potatoes out of the fire. They still had a crunch to them. I'm not sure if it was the gnawing hunger or the four slices of cheese I melted into mine or maybe just the feeling of not being quite so alone, but that was the best thing I'd eaten in a very long time.

# NIGHT SIXTEEN

IT WAS SO COLD I seriously considered wearing every pair of socks I'd brought. That, however, would mean leaving the safety of the sleeping bag, so I rolled around restlessly instead. I curled in on myself like a roly-poly. I forced my knees up under my shirt and my arms down my pant legs. With my head buried under the covers, I pulled my hands free again and held them to my ears. But it was no use. Nothing helped.

Outside the tent, the fire pit still glowed warm with embers. I arranged the logs back into a pile, trying my best to copy-cat Jason's order-in-chaos method. It didn't look the same, but I had to try. I leaned my face toward the coals and blew. The fire gasped. It sucked up each breath I gave it, glowing bright for a moment before dimming again. But my fire CPR was too sloppy. All I managed to do was blow flecks of soot into the air. The black snow storm wafted up in a circle and vanished into the night sky. The fire was dead.

I sat on my rock and stuck my feet next to the embers, letting them thaw. It wasn't much relief from the cold, but at this point I would have had to set myself on fire in order to warm up again. A trip to Venus was sounding pretty good about now.

I looked up, but it was far too late in the night to see our sister planet. With the blanket hugged tightly around my shoulders, I counted stars until I lost track of which ones I'd already given a number to and which were still waiting patiently.

While I counted, unaware, a swarm of ember fairies awoke. They fluttered out of the fire pit, nipping at me in their haste to rise up to the sky. The fire was returning to life. I had done it. I had created these flames. I had brought this creature back from the brink of death, and it now rewarded me with its generous heat. This was my fire.

I pulled my shoes out of the way and stomped them into the dirt. The heat came up through the soles and, though it was too dark to tell, they'd been burned black.

I turned my eyes up to the sky again. Tiny orange and red embers circled my head, thanking me for the gift of life. They floated up until they were indistinguishable from the stars. Above us, Mars glowered down, its steady twinkleless light almost audible in the still night air. The planet always seems to sing to me, like a siren. When I look at it, I get the strangest sensation that I'm upside-down, watching it from above, one stumble away from falling down and down off the Earth and down and down into the Red Planet's thin atmosphere and then down even further into the deep gorges of the Valles Marineris. I didn't trust Mars but I wanted so badly to dive into the sky after it. And if I wasn't weighed down by cold skin and hot, melted Keds, I might have.

Breaking my transfixion with our neighbor planet, I turned my attention back down to the flames. They glowed equally as red and aggressive as they greedily consumed the pieces of forest I fed them. Faces appeared in the coals, glowing melted-iron red. These fire faces had hollow black eyes and hungry, gaping mouths. I wouldn't mention them to Jason. He would only see them and worry. How could he not?

I bashed each face with the poking stick just as soon as I saw it. Sometimes two or three popped up at once, rising from the embers, forcing my stick down again and again. Some of them whistled at me when I snuffed them out and some popped in an explosion of sparks that jumped at me, as if they were trying to attach their hollow faces to my clothes and hair and grow in size and hunger there.

I should not have brought this fire back to life. It was too strong for me. I could never contain all its faces with just one stick.

I smashed another face in. And another. The fire retaliated, pulling at my stick and launching a surprise attack by grafting itself onto it. I shook my stick to get it loose, but the fire held fast. I pounded it against the stones, tried to break off the contaminated piece, but my stick broke open and spilled its burning orange insides onto the ground. The fire's cancer had travelled far up into the heart of it. It was too late now. I abandoned my only weapon to the enemy.

Above me, Mars laughed.

# DAY SEVENTEEN

WE ZIPPED ACROSS THE FLAT disk of the high plateau, past cattle and sheep and horses grazing at five thousand feet. Mountains jutted up around us like the worn-down teeth of a monster who takes eons to close his mouth. We could have made it all the way to Jason's next destination, we could have made it easily, but when the highway signs announce that Weed is just twenty-two miles ahead, you veer toward Weed.

I pulled off the highway and into the quaint downtown, where a tattered, wooden sign punned, "Weed Like to Welcome You." There was no other fanfare to mark our arrival. In fact, the town seemed to have shut down years before. The storefronts along Main Street were all for sale or lease. Even the bars had been boarded up and left for dead. A few lonesome ghosts wandered through town, on their way to or from the gas station liquor store for some day drinking to break up the monotony.

This used to be something. This used to be someone's dream. These used to be someone's homes and businesses and lives. Even the bakery, proud that it had been established all the way back in 1906, had bit the dust, the ovens sold, the logo chipping away. The only people who come here now are wayward travellers, and just for the joke that is this city's name.

At the railroad tracks, I turned the bike around. We found ourselves a room in an empty motel, dropped our things off, and headed out on foot. A few hippy-types pointed us toward a coffee shop that was still open. It was something.

Jason and I buzzed on double caramel white chocolate mochas and pretended we knew how to play chess. When Jason's horse flew across the board and knocked my king right over, I admitted defeat and retired to the sanctuary of the sofa.

I picked up a local newspaper that looked as though I could have printed it myself. There was a sad story about a lost Labrador puppy and an editorial condemning big business. "Stay Out, Starbucks!" it said, though rather pointlessly.

"The Weed Historic Lumber Town Museum opened back up for the season recently. We should check it out. It features sawmill machinery and artifacts from the pioneer days." Jason was reading the opposite side.

I lifted an eyebrow but played along. "Oh, boy!"

"Sawmill machinery!"

"Are you serious?"

"Yes!"

I tilted my head. It must have been hard to see the sarcasm in this light or something. "Tell me again if you're serious."

He'd already bounced up off the comfy couch. He had me by one arm, dragging me out onto the street. "I want to see the artifacts," he whispered, grinning like a kid pulling his mom toward his favorite animal at the zoo. Only he was a teenage boy pulling his friend toward archaic sawmill machinery.

I had to run down the sidewalk if I wanted to keep up with my arm.

Inside the museum it was 1887. The artifacts were a little spooky. Use had worn them more than time; you could see it in their age lines. As soon as we reached the first display, Jason and I parted ways.

There was something comforting to that. My experience with museums thus far had been limited to a handful of school field trips. Back then it had been necessary to stay in a group, holding hands with your buddy, feigning interest in each display for exactly as long as the teacher did. Now I was free to wander at my own pace, to fast-forward or to pause when I wished.

I breezed through the sawmill machinery, slowing my steps but never stopping. The old and still functioning (though I sure hope it wasn't the town's only) fire truck received the same half-hearted attention. What drew me in were the two rooms set up to look just like the rooms in a house from a hundred and some odd years ago. An iron, a real one, made of iron, perched on the stove ready to go. It had a smooth wooden handle that had been worn down through two generations of strong women's hands, hands that had been far stronger than mine. Their feet had worked hard too. The brown and black sewing machine in the corner had a foot pedal that worked in each stitch individually. Even the automation of production was the labor of human beings back then. There were no robots to complete the work. We had to do it ourselves.

My favorite artifact was the fire extinguisher. It had never been used. It was a glass ball, filled with water, that attached to the wall with a metal casing. When the extinguisher got too hot, the casing would let it drop, smashing it open and putting out the fire. But it only held about a pint. It couldn't put out more of a fire than an 1880's woman could have with the lid of a frying pan or with one carefully aimed whack of a kitchen towel. So much genius and engineering skill had gone into such a useless object.

I tried to imagine my bedroom on display like this a hundred years from now. Which of my precious objects would survive through the years? Would my Star Wars alarm clock, the one that looks like Boba Fett, last that long? Or would the paint chip off so that he looked just like any other anonymous snorkeler? Would the people of the future understand its function in a world where timekeeping devices are implanted directly into our brains? How about my mother's old diary, the one I stole? Would it be an enigma? How would the people of the future know how to read it? We ought to build them a Rosetta stone: English and Java and C++ carved on a monolith big enough that we couldn't lose it.

I must have been standing there for a long time because the next thing I knew, Jason was standing beside me ready to leave. I shook my head to banish the dreaminess.

"They're closing," he whispered. "Come on."

I took his hand, and we returned to the present. It was dusk, which startled me, like leaving a movie theater after a matinee and expecting the world outside to be as dark as the world inside had been. White birds whisked through the cool evening, flitting from streetlight to streetlight. I held up my hand to one and was surprised when it didn't fly away. It continued its impossible journey into the light bulb.

"Are these moths?" I asked, pulling Jason to a stop in the doorway of the pizzeria.

"Wow. Looks like it."

Knock, knock. It flew into the glass again and again, disregarding all evidence that it would never get inside that light.

"If you ever were to succeed at your task," I whispered to it, "you would die."

"Okay. Come on, Gandalf."

Jason's hand was still in mine, and he pulled me into the restaurant, my eyes lingering on the white moth at the lamp.

# NIGHT SEVENTEEN

The restaurant was poorly lit. I had to squint to make out the cats' faces in the gray metal cages on the back wall. There were a lot of cats for one restaurant. One large cage in the far corner even had what appeared to be a cheetah inside, but I couldn't be sure. The diners, oblivious to the animals or simply indifferent to them, ordered their meals, shared bites with friends, and sipped on red wine.

"Table twelve needs you," the waiter said to me. Not knowing what he meant, I ignored the call to action.

Instead, I approached one of the cages and pressed my fingers in between the bars. The yellow tabby arched her back and rubbed her body against the door. Her skin was warm beneath her slick fur. I pet her as best I could with just the tips of my fingers.

The lights flickered, just for a moment, and in the darkness I saw something. Some other world behind or underneath or beyond this one. But it was gone as soon as the light returned. I had only caught a glimpse of it.

If only I had more time.

"Table twelve," the waiter repeated, blocking my retreat with his broad shoulders and crossed arms.

"I'm not—"

"Everyone else is doing their job. You need to do yours."

He moved away again before I could protest.

Examining the table closest to me, I searched for numerical clues. Nothing under the corner of the table cloth. Nothing underneath the table. Nothing stamped on the back of the legs.

I brought my head back up from under the table, smiling at the astonished guests. They had ended their conversation somewhere in the middle in order to gawk at me. One held a fork halfway between the plate and her mouth.

"These tables," I tried to explain, "they're not numbered."

The woman shook her head and averted her eyes. I shouldn't have spoken to her.

I stepped back to give her some space and scanned the room in search of someone who might need me. No one seemed to need anything. The tables were full of food and the customers were full of smiles and conversation. Everyone was in good company. Well, everyone except for me and the cats.

The angry waiter caught me in his sight again. He loped over from across the room, weaving around the tables expertly, an intricate dance I lacked the coordination to copy.

I stood glued to the ground and his mouth grew so wide with the oncoming shout that I was sure he was about to swallow me whole. I stuck my fingers into one of the cages. The cat inside licked them.

And then the earthquake hit. The floor rose in waves beneath my feet, bouncing the plates and bottles off the tables. The diners executed an expert duck and cover, and I bolted for the door. Outside in the moonlight, I followed the side of the building until I stood face to face with the source of the earthquake.

The back of the restaurant pressed up against a lake, so close that the waves splashed along the wall. Across the water, maybe a quarter mile away, stood a tall, thin erupting volcano. Its precarious precipice curved in an arc as smooth as the crescent moon above. The bowl filled to overflowing with lava, red, red lava, which drooled down from its opened mouth. Its steep sides glowed in the light of its own blood.

The cats. They were locked in their cages. I couldn't leave them.

I sprinted back into the now empty restaurant. There were so many of them, so many cages. There wasn't enough time to unlock them all. I couldn't save them. I'd die in the attempt.

One then. I ran to the cage in the far back corner, the one with the cheetah in it, and let her out. The remaining cats were curiously quiet as they watched me follow the cheetah out the door to safety.

I ran as hard as I could, knowing that there was little chance for escape. But I would not be frozen in ash in a posture of surrender for all the future to see. No, they would find my pumice body with legs wide in a sprint and head up. When my feet splashed down into water, I dove in and swam equally as hard and fast. I swam out into the center of the lake; my arms aching, my head empty.

Then I looked up.

I'd done this wrong. Somehow in the confusion and the panic I'd gotten turned around and I'd been swimming as fast as I could toward the volcano. It loomed up larger from here. I'd halved the distance it seemed, in my haste.

I stopped and treaded water. There was no way to escape now. I could already see the shock wave coming toward me. The water bubbled and rose up in a great wave, and I just floated there and watched it. There was nothing else I could have done.

When it hit, I felt each molecule split apart, like I was breaking down into atoms and protons and quarks and then smaller and smaller to nothing.

Everything went dark for a moment and then became very bright.

I floated through the brightness, a non-corporeal fetus tucked in on myself like a ball. I had no thoughts and no judgments. I just was, floating there.

It was a full three hours before I finally woke up in a motel room in Weed.

# DAY EIGHTEEN

Jason worked out all the details before I woke up. He was already packed and he'd left the credit card slip perched neatly on the pillow next to me awaiting my signature.

"Hey! There she is. Come on, we have to hurry if we're going to make it there in time."

"Mmmm." I rolled onto my stomach. All those hours floating around in that bright light had worn me out.

"Come on. Get up, get up."

"Can I take a shower?"

"You won't need it where we're going."

"Where are we going?"

"The coolest place ever."

"Oh," I said, but I wasn't convinced.

I humored him anyway; let him point the way. We rode for a few hours, past lazy mountain towns and through groves of scarred, burnt-out pine trees. And then I learned where he was taking me.

At the sign, I skidded to a stop and stepped off the bike, pointing one finger at the offending word. My free hand plucked off my orange safety goggles, and I turned back to Jason shouting, "Does that say *Volcanic* National Park?"

Dazed, Jason climbed off the bike, fiddling with the keys to kill the engine. I'd left it running. There was no way we were staying.

"*VOLCANIC* National Park?" I asked again, louder this time and closer to his face. I had the start of a fight in my voice.

"Are you okay?"

My hands shook. My stomach tied itself into a knot. If I could have burned a hole in the sign with my eyes, I would have. "Why are we going into a volcano?"

Suddenly very close, Jason grasped one hand tightly against each of my shoulders, holding me up, keeping me from sinking into a reservoir of magma. "It's not going to explode."

"But it's a volcano."

"So what. We live on a giant fault line. There are tsunamis in the ocean and tornadoes in the middle of the country and meteors fall from the sky."

I tried to swallow but my throat was too sticky. "You don't understand."

"What don't I understand?" He didn't let me turn away.

"I..." I couldn't tell him. It was too crazy. He wouldn't get it.

"Tell me."

"My dream."

"What dream?"

"I dreamt I was killed by a volcano."

"So?"

"So it happened last night."

"So?"

So? How was I supposed to answer that? My mind chased its tail, frantically and pointlessly. It didn't make sense out loud.

"You're not supposed to die in a dream," I tried to explain.

"Says who? Lots of people dream about dying."

"But they wake up." I couldn't stop the soft tears that dripped from my eyes. I was sinking, and he wasn't going to be strong enough to pull me up.

"Yes," he confirmed. "And so did you." His hands still hugged my shoulders.

"But not until after."

"After what?"

The words squeaked out faintly. "After I died. After I was dead."

Touching the tip of his nose to mine, Jason wrapped his hands in a circle around my entire being. "But now it's over. You woke up and it was just a dream and now you're here with me. Let's go inside the park. Nothing's going to happen. You're okay."

"How do you know?"

"How do I know?"

"Yes, how do you know something horrible won't happen?"

"Well, I guess I don't. But I do know that this place is no more or less safe than any other place. Life is dangerous. That doesn't mean you stop living. Well, except for that one time, at the end."

I punched him in the shoulder. "Don't make me laugh. I'm serious."

"So am I. You can't worry about everything. You have to let go of some of it." His lips brushed up against my cheek. "And besides. I had a dream last night that you and I climbed the cinder cone and had a great time. We didn't die. We didn't even twist our ankles."

I didn't believe him about the dream but I nodded into his shoulder anyway. I let him lead us further up the mountain but I couldn't abandon all my fears at the sign on the side of the road. I carried them up with me, and they were so heavy that my tires pressed a rut into the pavement.

After we set up camp, Jason pulled me along the path that led to the cinder cone. Though I watched the scenery suspiciously, I followed after him. The cinder cone looked like nothing more than a pile of loose stones, the kind left at construction sites by big dump trucks. The trail wound up along its side at a steep angle, though the distance to the summit wasn't far.

Despite a climb of only a quarter mile, it was the most arduous hike I'd ever attempted. Each step I took brought me almost the same distance back down again as the baseball-sized cinders tumbled away beneath my shoes. I felt like I was inside a math problem. I was the frog in the well, hopping toward freedom and slipping back down each night as I slept. Each minute Artemis walks up three feet and slides down two. If the mountain is 800 feet from base to summit, when will she reach the top? This was going to take forever.

Three quarters of the way up, my legs quit. Just gave up. The end.

Jason was still climbing but he stopped when he could no longer hear the crunch of my footsteps behind him. He turned to me. "Come on. We're almost there. I can see the top."

"I can't." I had let my body sit down and it wasn't going to get back up without a fight.

He slid down the cinders to meet me and grabbed hold of one arm. "Nope. Not good enough. You are going to conquer this volcano. Now, up."

Though he managed to get me to my feet, the stones beneath us rolled away and we slid a little further down the mountain. His hand was wet in mine. Under normal circumstances I would have pulled away to remove the foreign body fluid, but up here I didn't seem to mind. My legs burned with each step I took, hand in hand with Jason.

When we reached the caldera and I did not find a pit of bubbling lava, I turned to him, held his face in both my hands, and kissed him inside the volcano.

# NIGHT EIGHTEEN

After spending a night freezing our noses off, we learned that plenty of wood is far from enough. When we got back from the cinder cone, we took the bike out to collect more.

"Log!" I shouted, for it was my turn.

I skidded to a stop, and Jason and I leapt from the bike, running madly in opposite directions. I headed toward the fallen log and half carried, half dragged it back. Jason scooped up an armful of small sticks and kindling, and deposited them in the sidecar along with my log. I hit the gas the instant our shoes left the pavement, and we zipped off down the road, resuming the hunt.

"Log!" Now it was Jason's turn.

Again we screeched to a halt, Jason sprinting in the direction he was pointing, me collecting as many small sticks as I could carry. In this manner, we filled the sidecar with as much wood as it could possibly hold, plus one log that rode back to camp on Jason's lap. We discussed the possibility of a second log run, but the minute we got back our legs gave out and our stomachs protested noisily. Jason got the fire started, and I wandered a little ways from camp where I found a large section of tree stump. It was far too heavy to carry, so I dragged it back to the fire.

"If we run out of wood," I suggested, "we can burn this." I patted my tree. You could have fit a Boy Scout troop on it.

Jason stopped huffing on the fire to give me and my tree a long, funny look.

"Yes?" I asked.

"That's a little, um, enormous."

"The better to feed the fire with, my dear," I said in my best wolf voice.

Jason shook his head. "Helicopters would have to put out our campfire."

"Hmm."

"I can't imagine that wouldn't come with a fine."

"It would probably come with a headline as well: Local Area Teens Burn Down Volcano. I kind of like the sound of that."

"Or maybe it would read: Runaway Teens Die in Tragic Forest Fire."

I laughed and skewered a turkey dog onto the end of a stick. Jason did the same and sat down beside me.

Quiet snuggled around us.

"I'm glad you came."

"I am, too."

"Would you have kept following me? If I kept going? If I couldn't ever go back?"

"Not forever."

Fairytale romances wouldn't approve of his response, but I did.

We fell back into a comfortable silence as the trees sucked up the last of the day's light through pine-needle straws. If you could peel their bark away quick enough, you might be able to catch a glimpse of the light they feed on. They keep it snug beneath their skin. I know because bits of it sometimes escape in the fire: a snap, a tiny explosion, a burst of light that returns to the sky to turn the stars on one by one.

Jason checked on his dinner and, unsatisfied, returned it to the flames.

"So," he asked, "what are you going to do when you get home?"

"Do you mean, 'Will it just be business as usual?'"

"Is that what I sound like?"

I laughed. "No, that's just my business voice. I use it when I say the word business or pretend to be a businessman. Also, I think it's the same voice I use for robots."

"The kind that assemble cars or the Asimov kind?"

"Definitely the Asimov kind, but, you know, before they abandon their programming and go on a killing spree. The kind that put cars together sound like this." I transformed myself into a robot for him, screwing in bolts and assembling the frame of an imaginary car. When the robot noises came out of my mouth carrying a spray of saliva with them, I collapsed into a laughing fit in my lap.

It was a few minutes before I regained myself and seriously considered his question. I took a bite out of my turkey dog and poked a fire-face in the eye with the same stick I'd cooked it on.

"I guess," I said softly, "I guess I'll learn to play the bass."

"What? The bass?"

"Yeah. That's what I'm going to do when I get home."

"That's not exactly what I meant, but okay. Why learn the bass?"

"Duh, Jason. Because everyone and their mother plays the guitar. Chicks that rock bass are way more kickass than girls that play guitar."

Jason smiled and stabbed the fire with his now empty stick. A slurry of sparks escaped into the sky. Was there a face he had to get rid of too?

"What do you want to be when you grow up?"

His question caught me off guard. "I don't know. An art professor?"

"Bullshit. That's what you tell adults. What do you really want to be?"

"Mm. Well. A colonist, I think."

"A colonist?"

"Yeah. I want to move to Mars."

"You wouldn't like it."

"Sure I would. I wouldn't have to put up with all the stupid stuff that happens in the world or any of the stupid people because all the Mars-people are going to be super smart."

"There's one problem."

"What?"

"Even if you escape to another planet you'll still never escape yourself."

A rock appeared in my throat. I tried to swallow it, but it wouldn't budge.

"You're your own worst enemy, you know."

"Yeah. So I've heard." I stabbed the fire again. "What about you? What do you want to be when you grow up?"

His answer took a while to form. "Kind," he said at last.

"That's such a cop-out answer. You already are. That so doesn't count."

"It does, too. People forget to be kind all the time. That's what happened to my parents. And I don't want that to happen to me."

"I wouldn't worry about it."

I erased the distance between us, pressing one whole side of me into Jason. His hand brushed across my back and came to rest against my hip. The edges of my shirt and jeans did not quite meet, and in that sliver of unclothed space his skin sparked fire into mine.

We leaned into one another. We fell.

There was no need for breath anymore. He provided all the air I could want. I might have stayed under indefinitely.

But somewhere in the middle of it all, Jason softened his hold on me to whisper, "I love you," across my lips.

"What?" I pressed my hand against the center of his chest, stopping him, stopping this. "What?"

For the longest minute of my life, Jason Messenger sat next to me and did not move farther away or closer in. At last he spoke again, but not to clarify or take it back, just to repeat: "I love you." This time there was no confidence in his voice.

I shook my head and pushed him another inch from me. "You can't."

He didn't close the space. "But I do."

I pushed him again, this time a little further. "Well, you can't."

"I don't understand."

"You're not the right one." My head was spinning. I was saying it wrong.

"What?"

I'm not the right one, Jason. I'm a trash compactor. I'm a black hole. I am the car graveyard. I ruin everything that comes too close.

I couldn't say it. I lied instead. "I don't want this."

"You do."

"You shouldn't have followed me here."

"You can't tell me that you don't feel this."

"I don't."

"Then why did you come back for me?"

"Tommy wasn't home!" The words erupted from my mouth, burning everything around. My ears were ringing so loud it sounded like glass breaking.

"Is that true?"

It wasn't. I was just wielding the T like a sword, like it was something to cut him with.

"I can't move any farther away from you."

I looked down at my hand. I guess I was still pushing him. I pushed harder, so hard that I flew off the other edge of the log and careened out into the darkness of the forest. If only gravity had been lighter, I could have kept spiraling away forever.

# DAY NINETEEN

When I returned to camp, my legs were wobbly, my hands were frozen, and Jason was asleep. I pulled my bed all the way to the far side of the tent but I guess it hadn't felt far enough because I woke up with my back pressed against the canvas and my shoulder digging into the cold ground. The bed lay in front of me like an inflatable shield.

In the morning, Jason packed up the tent in silence. I sat on the log poking the ashes with a stick. I didn't help at all. I didn't even let the air out of my bed. Once he'd arranged everything neatly into the sidecar, he came up behind me.

He didn't say anything.

I let him stand there.

Finally, he cleared his throat softly. "Ready?" he asked.

"In a minute."

I stirred the ashes around, waiting for the boredom to become insufferable.

Jason paused a moment more and then said, a little louder, "Let's go."

"Yeah, in a minute."

In my own time, I stood up, brushed the dirt from my clothes, and climbed onto the bike. Jason slid behind me carefully so that no part of him lent me any warmth. He held the back of the seat, and I pulled out onto the winding road.

We didn't have to talk; we could have rode in silence the whole way back.

"I don't know what happened," Jason said, louder than he needed to. "I don't know what I did wrong."

I refused to answer.

He wouldn't let it go. "It's okay if you're scared."

"I'm not scared."

"It would be okay if you were."

"Well, I'm not."

"Fine."

"Yeah." I gripped the handlebars as tight as I could.

"You're allowed to be happy, Artemis."

"Mmm-hmm." Color drained from my knuckles. My fingers tingled with the lack of oxygen.

"Why don't you want to be?"

"Why would you ask me something like that?"

"Because it's obvious that you don't. Because it's like you're set to self-destruct even though there aren't any Romulans invading the bridge—"

"I don't speak Star Trek."

"You do, too. You know exactly what I mean. And you don't have to be this way. You don't have to tear this apart. You don't even know if this could work because you won't give it a chance. You don't give anything time to grow, and then…then you complain that there's nothing in your life but dirt."

"You're mixing your metaphors."

"God. See? It's like you can't even hear me. And it's not like I'm saying that we belong together or that we'd live happily ever after or anything, but you won't even give it a chance. You can't run forever. You're going to fall off the edge of the map."

"Yeah, I think they proved that the Earth is a sphere."

"Well, then you're going to wind up back where you started. And what's the point of that? What's the point of running and running if you never get anywhere? What's the point of being alive if you won't stop and live every once in awhile?"

"I'll remember that the next time I'm walking across an overpass."

"Jesus. That's not what I meant."

The road was still looping down the side of the mountain. I hit a turn too hard, and Jason grabbed me by the hips.

"You're not going to fall off if you don't hold on, you know," I hissed.

"What?"

I tried to shrug myself away. "I said let go."

His hand had slid up under my shirt, not because he was trying to touch me, just because he was trying to hold on. But I didn't want him to. I threw his hand aside as if it were a spider, something grotesque that made my skin crawl. By the time I saw the little red lights it was too late.

We were still barreling down the road, but the car in front of us had already come to a complete stop. There wasn't time to slam on the brakes. I banked to the right, leaning the bike down onto its side and bending the sidecar mount until it broke. Jason and I were thrown clear. We landed in the dirt and pinecones. The bike slid a little farther down the shoulder before it too skidded to a stop. The sidecar, free at last, made a break for it and rolled down the side of the mountain, tumbling along until it reached the river a hundred yards below. Oblivious to everything but the music it blared and the chipmunk it had braked for, the car sped off.

I picked myself up carefully. My right pant leg had been ripped to shreds and the skin on my leg had been scraped off. It looked bad but it wasn't. Jason stood on the side of the road, his eyes on the sidecar at the bottom of the mountain. He was pale but uninjured. I stared a hole into him.

"This is your fault," I yelled as I ran down to the river.

The mount was bent in on itself and one of the wheels was nearly folded in half. I kicked the sidecar and I kicked the stupid tent that lay next to it.

Jason was already by my side. "Can we fix it?"

"No, we can't fix it," I shouted. "Look at it."

"Well, we can't just leave it here."

"What do you propose we do?"

"What about all the stuff?"

"I can't carry it all." I couldn't; I left it all behind and tromped up the hill.

Jason wavered for a moment in front of the sidecar before grabbing his backpack and following me. Some of the paint had been scratched off the side of the bike but besides that it seemed to be okay.

"Idiot," I said.

I'm pretty sure I would have left Jason there at the base of the volcano if he hadn't jumped on behind me.

# NIGHT NINETEEN

FOUR SUMMERS AGO, PRINCE AND I went to visit Grandma, and she taught me how to bake a cake. As it turns out, I'm not half bad at it, just don't ask me to bake any cookies. My mad cake-making skills just don't seem to translate.

I found myself at home, in the kitchen, *Betty Crocker Cookbook* propped against the windowsill, cake in progress. The recipe directed me to separate the eggs. Grandma had taught me how to do that with my hands, not with the eggshell. The eggs don't break in your hands, and I like the way they feel anyway, slimy and soft and not without substance.

I hit an egg on the inside of the sink until the white leaked through the cracks a little. Then I pulled at the shell to break it in two, cupping the egg in my hand, holding onto the yolk and waiting for the last string of white to finally let go and come down with a plop in the bowl. Each time I got an egg separated though, the yolk would suddenly deflate, leaking orange and yellow into the egg whites. So I poured the ruined egg out into the sink and tried again.

And again. And again.

Hours later I looked around and realized I was surrounded by mountains of broken, empty eggshells, and I was pouring egg after egg down the drain.

# DAY TWENTY

I dropped Jason off at the bus station. He would call his mom to pick him up and wouldn't have to lie to her about what happened because she wouldn't want to hear about his trip. She'd be happy to have him back. Not that I cared.

On my way out of the station, I reached inside my wallet, removed the credit card, and bent it back and forth until it snapped in two. One half I threw away, the other I returned to my wallet, sliding it behind the movie stubs.

I climbed back on the bike and turned toward my former life. As was so often the case, I would return from the journey so changed that I could barely recognize myself. Everyone else would still be the same. I'd have to straddle that gap between parallel universes alone. Again.

I turned onto my street. This moment is clear in my mind. The rest is hazy, as if I were watching it through murky water.

My house was framed in gray—clouds above and grass below all one hue. There was no blue and no green to break up the lines of the scene, just grasshousesky.

I parked the bike out front, hearing the rustle of the pink paper before I saw it. My eyes were busy elsewhere, searching for the missing dead cars. Each had left its brown shadow behind, and I was trying to remember who went where. Was this one the Camaro or the Viper? Did I hear the engine turn over once in this spot, or was it over there, behind the house? My feet walked up the stairs automatically. My hand reached out to grab the doorknob.

Locked.

The pink paper flapped to me.

I reached out for it; ripped it away from the door. A corner still clung beneath the tape, but the rest pulled away so easily that I was surprised the wind hadn't already shredded it into a million pieces.

"No..." the torn corner said to me, englossed by tape and still stuck firmly to the door. "No..."

I don't think I was breathing, or, if I was, the air was thick like water. No, thicker. Like colorless Jell-O.

I didn't need to read the rest.

"No..."

Nobody will let you in. No one lives here. Now you are alone. Nothing is left. No... No...

"No... tice of Eviction," the paper in my hand told me calmly, without judgment or anger.

Just simply,

Notice of Eviction.

# PART THREE

# NIGHT TWENTY

Without me, there was nothing to stop our home from shriveling up like a corpse in the desert. Its walls sucked up against its vacant rooms, bowing inward, emaciated, empty of humanity. The eviction notice was a scab on the dry, cracked lips of the door. 7843 Locust Street begged for water, for nourishment, for affection. It drank my tears deliriously.

For hours I circled, dragging my fingertips across each board, smearing blood, tears, dirt, and soul into the house in rings that wouldn't stick. Around and around I went, a mindless shark, unable to fill the gaping hole in my heart. When my awareness finally awoke and I looked up into the sky, an orange moon stared solemnly down, hidden in part behind a mask of thin clouds. My fingers had been worn to bloody stumps. I felt nothing.

I tore at the seams of the windows and doors but every single point of entry had been locked tight against me. I could still see shadows of our furniture behind the flimsy, yellowed curtains. Shut away.

If Walker were bigger, I could have snuck down into his burrow with him. We would pass the long hours of the night held tight in each other's arms, enveloped in the good soil. Our hearts would grow back some of the roots that had been stripped away, and we would start to heal. But Walker wasn't having me; I couldn't even find his hole.

I lay down on my back in the center of Prince's garden. The baby carrots had just burst up from the ground, and I swept my hand in a circle over them, feeling each one bend beneath me before springing skyward again.

My eyes burned each time I blinked, as if my eyelids were coated in sandpaper. I gave up, turned over, and left them closed.

The cool of the earth seeped into every inch of me, dousing the fire in my cheeks and stomach, giving me some small measure of relief. It would have been so easy. Just stop, that's all. Just stop moving forward. Just lie down and bury your head in the garden. Flesh to earth. As natural as anything. I rubbed my cheek against the dirt, exploring the option.

But I couldn't stop my heart. It raced, faster and faster, even as I begged it to stop. It beat against me so hard it hurt, so hard I was sure it was going to explode and all the blood would burst out into the dark, unexplorable expanses of my body.

An orange fire glowed from behind my closed eyes, emitting a searing heat despite the chill on the garden floor. I smelled metal and burning tires and I choked on the stench of it. I couldn't breathe. I couldn't rest. I opened my salt-sticky eyes again.

The moon had shifted in the sky. Now it hovered just above the horizon, swelling to twice its normal size. I had not slept, I was sure, but it seemed I had shut my eyes against many hours. I turned onto my back again. Large drops of rain had begun to tumble from the sky—slowly gaining momentum.

I held my eyes open to the rain and let it seep into me. It dripped in through my tear ducts and flowed through my veins, leaving behind the same grime it leaves on cars the day after you wash them.

Run your fingers across my skin and you'll come away with ash.

# DAY TWENTY ONE

I WOKE IN THE POURING rain with my face under the zucchini plant. My hands were so numb I couldn't close them all the way. Shaking, I pressed them into sloppy fists, squeezing them open and closed again and again, but they moved only reluctantly. We read "Rip Van Winkle" in school once. He'd slept for a hundred years. I knew how he felt.

The rain had washed all traces of dirt, blood, and tears away. I raised my face into it, stripped off my cold, clingy clothes, and showered in the garden beneath the sky.

With nothing clean to change into, I wrung out the outfit I'd just crawled out of and climbed back inside. My shirt twisted itself around, refusing to fit straight. My jeans suctioned onto my knees, uncomfortably close. They sported a hole from when we fell off the bike but they were all I had.

I didn't have anything to do so I wandered into the front yard to play with my memories. I sat in the shadow the Mustang had left behind and made soft vrooming sounds with my mouth. My hands were perched in the air at ten and two.

They pulled up behind me quietly. Sensing them, I checked my rearview mirror, but it was only imaginary and didn't yield an image. They exited their vehicle and floated out onto my road, coming up alongside and asking that I pull over. I killed the engine, put the car in park, and rolled down the window.

"I don't like cops," I blurted out. It surprised me too, and I quickly raised one hand to my mouth to cease whatever other nonsense it might betray me with.

The first cop laughed at the abruptness of my comment. The second lifted his shades off his eyes to make sure it was in fact this wet little girl sitting on the grass in front of him that had just dared to speak so freely.

I didn't follow up on my first attempt at a greeting except with a shrug. I lowered my hand from my mouth.

"How come you're not at school?" the "nice" cop asked in his kind voice.

"Teacher work day," I answered without a blink.

"Mmm-hmm. And where do you live?"

I pointed toward my neighbor's house, the one with the nice couple who'd moved in a few years ago. For a moment, I believed my own lie. I remembered sitting around the table with them in the evening, joking about the day and laughing so hard we couldn't swallow our tuna noodle casserole.

"So this isn't your yard?"

"It's the ghosts' yard. Look around, Cop." I stared at him. "Mr. Cop," I added, but that didn't sound right, either.

"Do you know who lives here?" he asked. His partner crossed his arms and examined the distance.

"The ghosts. No one. It's empty." I wouldn't tell them about Walker. He didn't deserve a pink notice of eviction.

"What school do you go to?"

"Lincoln." I didn't have a lie to give them.

"You need to go to school."

"I told you, it's a teacher work—"

"No, it isn't."

"I'm wet."

"Should have thought of that before you tried to ditch."

He closed his robot hand around my arm and lifted me through the roof of the shadow car. I wasn't handcuffed, but they threw me into the plastic backseat cage anyway and drove me the mile and a half to school.

"We're letting you off with a warning this time," my new friend informed me, opening my door. "Next time we'll have to ticket your parents. You don't want that, do you?"

I took in a breath to respond to this inane threat and held it there on the back of my tongue for a long moment before deciding that the only course of action was to exit the vehicle and walk into the office.

I had no idea what time it was. I stood in front of the school secretary and waited for her to acknowledge me.

"Why so late this morning, Artemis?"

"Dentist appointment," I told her, my bangs dripping rudely on the counter.

"Do you have a note?"

"No, sorry. I forgot to get one."

She looked me up and down. "It's really coming down out there, huh? Your mother didn't give you an umbrella?"

"I—"

"Forgot." she added softly, shaking her head at me. "You want some extra gym clothes or something, honey?"

A kid like me, an outcast weirdo artist kid like me, should never ever wear clothing that displays the school's ridiculous mascot, but I was cold and I felt like a half-drowned mutt so I nodded.

It was warm inside the sweat pants and hoodie.

My slip read 10:37. I wondered if they would try to call my mother to excuse the tardy. Maybe they could give me her number.

I paused for a moment, but the secretary had taken a phone call so I went to science.

"Any questions?" Mrs. Haskell asked, accepting my note without a second glance.

I have lots.

Joey Krakowski raised his thick hand. "How long would it take me to die in space?"

*Why do you care? You're never going into space.*

Mrs. Haskell's eyes glittered like stars beneath her space-helmet glasses. "Well," she answered, puffing up her shoulders, "if you found yourself suddenly sucked into the vacuum of space, you could, if you hyper-ventilated first, filling each blood cell with as much oxygen as it could possibly hold, survive for up to a minute before your blood boiled and froze at the same time and the alveoli in your lungs all exploded." She acted out all the verbs.

But who cares? Exactly no people in this room are ever going into space. And if by some freak chance it turns out I'm wrong and dying in the eternal emptiness becomes a real possibility, I'm sure NASA can fill them in.

*Where do you go, Mrs. Haskell, when your house is taken away from you?*

Karen raised her hand next, her bracelets sliding down to her elbow. "How long could we survive if the sun disappeared?"

*That question doesn't even make any sense. Where's it going to go?*

"Well. That's a really interesting question. Were the sun somehow to mysteriously vanish, it would take us eight minutes to even find out."

The class blew out a collective, "Whoa."

"And then we would veer out of our orbit and go tumbling away through the galaxy. The planet would freeze over almost instantly as we careened out into the darkness."

"Cool!"

"Yes, Lucas."

"Can I go to the bathroom?"

Audible giggles.

"No. Yes, Desiree."

"What if the moon crashed into us?"

I collected my things.

"Miss Cato, please sit down."

"No," I told her. My tone was simple and direct, and I remained standing, hugging my books against my chest. "I can't stay here anymore. I need to go. I have something real to do."

"I assure you, Artemis, this is quite real."

"The sun disappearing, the moon crashing into us, and Joey getting sucked into space. These are not real scenarios."

"This is your education—"

"Then educate me about something I can use. I have to go."

I'm pretty sure she went on without me. At least, she didn't follow me into the hall or anything. I kept walking away from the classroom and all the way out of school in a straight, directionless line. Kind of like the earth given the sudden vaporization of the sun; freezing over and tumbling away into the darkness.

# NIGHT TWENTY ONE

I STOOD WITH MY NOSE against the glass for an hour watching Jason eat dinner with his mom. He was putting on a brave face for her but he wasn't happy. And it was my fault. I'd led him to the edge of a cliff and then shoved him off of it instead of climbing down with him. I'd pushed away the last person who mattered and there was no taking it back.

"What are you doing here? What do you want?" he said through the screen, standing with his back against the wall where I couldn't see him.

I didn't answer. I walked home so I wouldn't cry and when I got there, I curled up in the dirt and slept.

I SAT ALONE AT THE kitchen table reading the back of the cereal box. It didn't have any nutritional value of its own, so they'd had to enrich it with vitamins and metals and real foods. Ingredient the first: puffed corn. Ingredient the second: high-fructose corn syrup. Ingredient the third: corn starch.

Knock, knock, knock.

*That's funny. I'm not expecting anyone.*

I wafted over to the door and looked through the peephole, which I never do, but I couldn't see anyone. Curiosity beat out fear. I undid the deadbolt.

Jason practically flew into the house, knocking me aside on his way in. Eyes darting around wildly, he slid the door shut with his back and locked it up again.

"What's—"

But he cut me off with a finger to his lips and a quick shake of his head.

He continued to scan the room as he slid the chain lock into place by feel. I looked around, too, but uselessly since I didn't know what we were looking for.

Finally, satisfied that the locks were in place and that there was nothing to see here, Jason grabbed me by the wrist and dragged me into the back bedroom, the one my parents used to share once upon a time. He shut the door behind us and stopped my hand when I reached for the light switch.

"I don't know what you did," Jason panted in the darkness, "but you've got the Mob on your tail."

"The Mob?" I laughed. "That's ridiculous."

He must have been kidding me. I couldn't see his mouth well enough to make out the dim arc of a smile, though; all I could see were the whites of his eyes.

He was serious. "What did you do?"

"I don't know what you're talking about. What's going on, Jason?"

"Shit. I was hoping you could tell me that. The Mob doesn't put a hit on you for nothing, you know."

"I don't understand."

"Understand it or not, they're out there and they're after you."

The fear hit me all at once, like a train, followed swiftly by Jason who tackled me, knocking me down to the floor. I hit the wood so hard it knocked the wind out of me.

"You're hurting me," I coughed, both my hands trapped in one of his.

Jason yanked at my shirt, ripping it up over my bra as he pulled something long and shiny out of his pocket.

"Stop it. You're hurting me. Jason, stop."

"Hold still."

He pulled my shirt up over my face.

"If you just hold still it won't hurt as much."

He pressed the device in between my ribs as hard as he could, as if he were trying to stab me with its blunt tip.

"Ow. Jason, stop."

It whirred to life, drilling a hole in my side and depositing a marble-sized metal bead beneath skin and muscle and bone.

"Shut up. Stop screaming. I need this if I'm going to be able to find you again."

He let me go. I sat up and pulled my shirt back down.

"What did you put in me?"

"A tracking device."

I rubbed my finger across the place he'd implanted it. I couldn't feel a hole or anything, but it hurt like hell. In that moment, I wasn't sure I wanted him tracking me down, Mob problems or not.

"Artemis." Jason pulled me to my feet. "Listen to me. They're coming to rub you out. You'd better run."

"Come with me."

He laughed but just with his breath, and, for an instant, I saw him for who he really was.

Then I forgot, and he was Jason again.

"I'm not going down with you. You're on your own, kiddo."

A window in the living room shattered. They were inside the house. Jason threw open my parents' window and tossed me out into the car graveyard.

The grass was slick with rainwater. I crawled on my stomach, pulling myself through the shadows under a starless sky.

When I reached the Viper, I slipped underneath it to hide while I figured out my next move.

I was trapped. A man with pointy shoes was patrolling the yard.

He didn't see me, not yet anyway, but he strolled back and forth just a few feet in front of me, blocking any hope I had of making a break for it.

"She's not in here," a voice shouted from the house.

The pointy-shoe man stopped pacing and turned to face the voice. He lit a cigar. I couldn't see him do it, but I heard the click of the lighter and smelled the thick smoke rolling off him. "Oh, she's around," he purred. "Keep looking."

My heart was beating so hard I was sure it was going to give me away.

"Here, kitty, kitty, kitty. We know you're out there. Come out, come out."

He was so close I could have reached out and grabbed his ankles. If only I had a weapon, a sharp stone or something.

"Boo!"

He poked his bulbous nose under the car and reached two fat fists out to grab hold of me. I scurried out from under there so fast I swear I heard a boom like thunder as the air crashed in to fill the space I'd left behind. I raced down the street, down toward town.

"Get her! There she goes!" They shouted at my back, but I was too fast for them. I turned the corner and ducked into an abandoned building.

This used to be the Red Lynx Telecommunications warehouse. I'd come inside exactly four times on "Bring Your Daughter to Work Day." But the building had sat empty for years, crumbling away brick by brick.

I wasn't alone. Above me, in the office on the second floor, low voices rumbled something sinister.

I tiptoed up the stairs, dragging my hand through the dust that had settled on the rail.

“What do you want us to do with the boy?” the first voice asked.

“He’s not useful anymore,” the second one answered.

“He could be trained.”

“Nah. Not worth it.”

“I’ll call it in, then.”

He stepped out of the office right in front of me and his hand shot out so fast I didn’t even have time to think, much less run. He grabbed me by the throat, not so tight that I couldn’t breathe but too tight for me to speak.

“Lookie, lookie. Isn’t that lucky. Got myself a little pussycat by the tail.”

“Well, what do you know? Came right to us. All we had to do was sit back and wait.”

“Where do you want her, boss?”

“Give her to the driver.”

He lifted me right off the ground, carrying me down the stairs by the neck, and stuffed me into the trunk of a car. We drove for hours and when we finally stopped I was more bruise than skin.

At what I thought was the end of the road, Jason opened the trunk and reached inside to help me out.

“The tracking device,” I said. “But how did you get rid of the mobsters?”

He bit his lower lip. “I’m sorry,” was all he said.

“No. You don’t have any reason to be. I’m the one—”

But I was cut short when he pointed the gun at my chest and pulled the trigger.

# DAY TWENTY TWO

When I woke, the sky was the shade of gray that makes it impossible to determine the hour. No rain had fallen, though large glistening drops of water blanketed the ground and rolled off the edges of the leaves.

My fingers were too stiff to straighten, but I wasn't cold anymore. I laid on my back and worked my hands open and closed as best I could. They moved like claws, like bear hands. Useless.

I sat up and immediately regretted it. My head was woozy, as if I hit it one too many times on the side of the trunk last night. The world wouldn't sit still; everything danced around along the edge of my sight. I checked the spot on my ribs where I'd dreamt that Jason stuck a tracking device into me. It was still sore.

Ignoring the pounding in my head, I stood, overcome by the feeling that something was very wrong. My hands, my eyes, my muscles, my joints. Nothing was working right.

I had grown old.

I ran my fingers across my face, searching for the deep lines I knew time had given me, but they were oddly absent. My skin retained its spring and smooth complexion. The night had only worn down the insides of me. I sat back down, and Walker hopped into the garden.

"You're still here."

*Of course I'm still here,* he didn't say. *I live here.*

"I thought you'd left us."

*You left us.* He wiped his eye with one of his paws.

"I didn't know, Walker. I didn't know that things were this bad."

He seemed to nod slightly, but I couldn't be sure.

Then he scratched his ear with his back leg and filled his mouth with dark green leaves.

My stomach snarled.

I wasn't sure if Walker and I could eat the same kinds of things, but I didn't know what any of the plants were and I wasn't likely to receive another guide. I grabbed a handful of the same leaf Walker was eating.

It was spinach. I ate, stuffing leaf after leaf into the bottomless hole that used to be my stomach. Then Walker hopped to another plant, and I ate that one, too. The long dusty-looking leaves tasted like peppery cabbage. They were better than the spinach. I quickly filled myself with this new leaf, my eyes on Walker all the while, watching to see what else was good.

He caught on quickly and took me on a whirlwind tour of the garden, nibbling small bits of everything eatable. I'd never been a fan of salad and eating my vegetables was often a struggle. This morning, however, they fulfilled every culinary fantasy I'd ever had, including the one about the ice cream-sundae-cake cookie-dough-bites.

After a half hour of gorging on leaves, I took my hands off the plants and laid back into the dirt, feeling as if I might explode into a family-sized salad. The urge to grab and pick and stuff was still there, but I forced myself to stop.

Walker continued to hop around and munch on his breakfast. Once, he came just close enough for me to touch, but when I reached my hand toward him in gratitude he scampered a few feet farther away.

The gray steamed off the sky, leaving behind a deep blue—at first in uneven patches and then all over.

"Well, Walker," I began, startled by the volume of my own whisper. "You seem to have things pretty good out here. How do you like living in the garden?"

He stared at me and stopped chewing, a spinach leaf poking out the side of his mouth.

"Walker, do you miss Prince? I do. I didn't know he'd be gone when I got back. They didn't even leave a note."

Walker continued chewing, his shiny brown eyes fixed on mine.

I covered my face with my hand.

Walker hopped closer and butted me in the cheek with his head but zipped away again when I reached up to pet him.

Then it hit me.

I got up, cleaned myself up as best I could, and ran the six blocks to Prince's school. Sure enough there he was, knocking a tetherball around and around its pole, missing twice for each good whack he landed. I approached from out of the shadows, my heart beating as fast as it could. Did he still hate me? What would he say?

"Artemis!"

"Hey, Prince."

He rushed over to me, threw his arms tight around my waist, and pressed his face uncomfortably hard against the sore spot on my ribs. He had forgotten my past transgressions, just like Jason said he would.

"Where were you?" he asked, muffled by my sweatshirt.

"Grandma's house."

"Did you bring me seeds?" He pulled back and his hands dug automatically into my pockets. But there wasn't anything in them.

"No, I didn't get any seeds."

"Oh." He was squirming away already, responding to the call to return to class.

I held onto him by one chubby wrist. He was cleaner than I'd ever seen him before. "Where's Mom?"

"Mom was 'rested. I live in Paul and Charlotte's house."

"Wait. What?"

He was slipping away, twisting his arm around to break my hold on him. I gripped down harder to forbid him his escape.

"She was arrested? What happened? Stay. You don't need to go to class right now."

He looked longingly toward his teacher who gathered the toddling kindergartners up like butterflies to her sweet flower print dress. I yanked Prince through the gap in the fence away from her. She would be counting up the children, checking to see if anyone had lingered in the garden. I didn't have much time before they would come out to look for him.

Still holding Prince roughly by the arm, I walked him down the sidewalk faster than his legs would go and steered him around behind a dumpster.

"Tell me what happened." I demanded, kneeling down to his level.

"I was in my room playing with my LEGOs and then there was a knock at the door. And I asked who is it and it was the police, so I let them in."

"You're not supposed to let the police in."

"Miss Amy says that the police are good guys and that they're there to help."

"Okay, fine. What happened when you let them in?"

"Well, the one man told me I was a good boy but that Mom was in trouble and then he gave me a cookie. It was a chocolate cookie. He let me eat it in the back of the car." He stopped as if that was the end of the story. Our mother was arrested and he got to eat a chocolate cookie in a police cruiser. He struggled again, his face pained, turning back toward school.

"What happened to Mom? What did she do?"

He shrugged. "Assault?"

"Who did she assault?"

He shrugged again. I could see his brain working overtime behind his eyes, trying desperately to figure out how our mother had gotten in trouble.

"Do you know how long she's in jail for?"

"She's in jail?"

"What did they tell you?"

"She's resting."

"They lied."

"Oh. Artemis, I'm glad you're home again."

"Me too. Where are you staying?"

"6-4-1-7 Pinecrest Place. With Paul and Charlotte. They have a dog. His name is Bandit."

"6-4-1-7?"

"Pinecrest Place."

"Okay. I'm going to come over tonight to talk to you some more. Watch for me, okay?"

He nodded.

"Go back to school. Tell your teacher you were talking to a squirrel and got carried away or something."

"But I'll get in trouble. I need a note."

"I can't write you a note. I'm incognito."

"But, Artemis, they'll make me turn my color. I'll go to blue."

"It's okay. Sometimes it's okay to get in trouble if it's for something important."

He implored me with his big watery eyes.

"I'll turn it back to green when I see you later. Now go."

Prince skipped off back through the fence, and his teacher collected him in the folds of her dress, her little lost butterfly.

I sunk down against the side of the dumpster and tried to slow the racing of my heart.

# NIGHT TWENTY TWO

My intention was to creep around the house, find Prince, and take him away with me. Step one was solid; I rehearsed it in my head while I rode to Pinecrest Place. As of yet, I hadn't developed a step two. I guess I figured I would think of something later.

But the front door of 6417 opened wide when I was still four houses away, and a pretty young woman in a teal shirt waved me the rest of the way in. Prince told them I was coming. I need to better explain to that boy the meaning of incognito.

The woman surrounded me with her warmth and kissed the side of my head. "Welcome, Artemis."

Prince, in turn, wrapped himself around her leg, one hand creeping steadily toward my pocket. "Did you bring me seeds?"

I shook my head, still partially immobilized by the stranger's embrace.

She led me into the house, introduced herself as Charlotte and her husband as Paul. I had a place at the table with a large empty plate, a small empty plate, a fork, a knife, and a glass of water. They'd waited to have dinner. I had no exit strategy from this fortress of tableware, so I accepted the wine glass full of apple cider and let them serve me lasagna and salad.

Prince, it seemed, had adapted well. He alternated bites, one from his main plate, one from the side, and kept a hand firmly grasped around one glass or the other at all times.

The silence was hot under the nervous gaze of Charlotte and Paul. They watched me, smiled, turned away, peeked up at me again. They didn't seem able to hold eye contact for any length of time.

"We heard that you ran away a couple weeks ago. We'd like for you to stay with us tonight," Charlotte said at last.

I arranged a bite of lasagna on my fork and raised it up to my mouth. I had nothing to say to her so I stuffed it in.

She smiled looking down at her own untouched dinner. "Prince is a wonderful little boy," she continued. "And we're happy to be here for him until your family gets things straightened out. We want you to know that we're here for you, too. You're safe with us. You don't have to run anymore."

I swallowed and swooshed a sip of cider around in my mouth, dividing my attention between squirming Charlotte and her silent husband.

"Well," I explained, "first of all, I didn't run away. I went on a road trip."

"A road trip?"

"Mmm. On my motorcycle. My friend and I rode to the coast and then up into Oregon. Second of all, my family has never been and never will be straightened out."

"What do you mean?"

"Well, our father left a couple weeks ago; walked out the door and didn't look back. No biggie, though, he hasn't been much of a father for years. Barely looks up from the TV." I was scaring her off. I continued recklessly. "My mother... my mother hasn't been sober since Prince was born. One time—this is hilarious—one time I came home from school. I was, maybe nine, and my mother had this steak that she was defrosting in the kitchen sink. The water was running and she held the steak in her hands under it and just stood there like normal; like nothing was wrong. Only, she was standing very, very still with her ear to her shoulder as if she was listening. I walked up behind her and was about to tell her about my day at school and then I realized that she had passed out. She was standing at the sink, holding a frozen steak, water running all over her and starting to pour down onto the floor, and she was passed out cold."

No one laughed. Paul and Charlotte paled, freezing to stone as if they sat across from a gorgon.

Prince glared at me. "Stop being aliens."

I kicked him under the table.

Charlotte and Paul snapped out of their trance.

"Being aliens?" It was Paul. His voice was different than I imagined it would be: lower and with more gravel in it.

"That's what she does. That's her goal in life. She aliens people."

"She *alienates* people," Paul recommended. I liked Prince's version better; it sounded like I had a ray gun that blasted people onto other planets. Pew. Pew.

"Well," Charlotte said, "you're not scaring us off. The offer still stands. We have a bed all made up for you and we really hope you'll stay."

But I don't follow directions well. I slipped out the window while Paul gathered the dishes and Charlotte scooped ice cream into pretty glass bowls.

"I'll be back for you," I whispered to Prince from the yard.

He smiled and waved.

Once, when I was very young, I wandered away from home and got lost. I remember toddling down an endless sidewalk, trying desperately to recall the details that distinguished my home from the rest of the world. A big brown door opened, and a woman stepped out onto her porch. She walked toward me, crouched down, and motioned with her arms that I should go to her. When, unafraid, I did, she lifted me high off the ground and, after squinting as far down the empty streets as her eyes would reach, she brought me into her house.

Inside, she sat me down on the counter and gave me a box of cookies, the circle kind that were really good when I was little but don't taste like much of anything anymore. She spoke to me kindly, asking my name and what my mommy and daddy looked like. I understood her all right but still lacked the language to answer, so I ate my cookies and shrugged a lot.

She called her neighbors. She called her friends. She called the police. She sent her husband outside to search for those who were searching for me while she kept me high up on the counter, calm, and warm, and well fed.

It couldn't have been long before she found my parents. They must have realized my absence quickly, and, on such short wobbly legs, I couldn't have gone far. My daddy came to pick me up, led inside by the nice woman's husband. He hugged me and kissed me and lifted me onto his shoulders and carried me home.

Only, this isn't the way it happened.

I did wander away when I was one and a half, but it was my mother who recovered me. A nice lady never found me and never gave me cookies. I was not gone for more than five minutes. I had simply gone for a walk and, when my mother looked up from her book, I was out of sight. I had followed a path around a grassy hill and strolled along looking at the daffodils. She caught up. I smiled at her and pointed to the flowers, and she took my hand and let me finish my walk before carrying me home again.

I don't remember this version of the story; the version she tells. I only remember the lady with the cookies and riding tall on my father's shoulders all the way back home. I should know there's something wrong with my story because in this memory the father who picks me up is not my father. He's some other man that I don't know. It must have been a dream.

But I can't convince myself that it didn't really happen.

# DAY TWENTY THREE

In the morning, it started to rain again. A storm had come in from Alaska and the droplets were like ice water. I wouldn't have lasted long in the garden so, with nothing better to do, I went to school.

I was late again, but this time the secretary didn't ask me why. She handed me some clean gym clothes and told me to change and then head over to my second period class. As soon as I stepped away, she picked up the phone. I guess the office was really busy that morning.

I changed and tiptoed into history twenty minutes late.

Miss Gonzales wasn't going to let me sneak in unnoticed. She wrapped up her lecture quickly and then told the class to get started on the evening's reading assignment. If they worked hard, she said, they might even be able to get their homework done in class. I sat at my desk with my head cast down onto the random page I'd opened my book to, imagining, like I used to when I was little, that if I couldn't see her she couldn't see me. No good. Once the class had started reading she pulled me into the hall for a more private conference.

"I heard about what happened in science the other day," she whispered.

"Talking about me behind my back, I see?" I quipped.

Her face drew into itself in a frown that made my vague attempts at sarcastic humor seem inhumane. Her eyes shimmered through a shield of water.

"No," she explained, the words catching in her throat. "It's… I… I'm worried."

I cringed. Two big tears collected in her eyes. They hadn't dropped yet. I had never made a teacher cry before. I didn't mean it.

"Don't worry," I told her. "I'm doing alright; just normal teenage stuff is all. You know, acting out against authority figures, talking back, staying up too late, playing violent video games."

"I don't believe you. This isn't normal teenage stuff. I'm really worried about you, Artemis."

"Is this really the best time to talk about this?" I was running on reserve fuel only.

"Will you stay after class and talk to me?"

"Yes," I answered, but by the time the bell rang I had already escaped down the hall.

On my way to science, the secretary caught hold of me.

"Hi, Artemis. Can you come back to the office with me? There's someone here who wants to talk to you."

I'd never seen her away from her desk before. I didn't even know she had legs.

"Who?"

"Just come back with me."

She gave me a look that let me know that she knew. They knew, they all knew. It was like I had a brand on my skin and everyone could see just what I was. I wanted to jump inside my locker to hide, but I couldn't squeeze myself down to twelve by twelve by fifteen. Instead, I swallowed the lump in my throat and followed the secretary down the hall.

"Hey, can we talk?" It was Jason. My head was spinning.

"Now's not a good time."

"It's never a good time. You know, you could stand to be a little less selfish."

The secretary put an arm between us. "Now's not a good time, Jason. You can talk to your friend later."

"Oh."

He stood there, mouth still open in an O-circle watching them lead me into the office as if condemned.

I was sent to the principal's office once in the third grade for biting another student on the hand. I wasn't afraid then but I was now because everyone else was, too.

I sat down. I felt like I was breathing underwater.

"Hello, Artemis. My name is Rick. I'm a licensed social worker and I'm here to help you."

I swallowed a wave of nausea.

"I hear that you ran away."

The blood just beneath my skin burned like acid.

"Yet, here you are at school."

He smiled. I didn't. I was waiting to dissolve into a puddle of slime.

He tried again, this time all-business. "I'd like to discuss what's been going on with you these past couple weeks. Where have you been staying?"

When I spoke, my voice sounded tinny, like a bad recording. "I didn't run away. I went to my grandmother's house. I just needed some time to work some things out."

"Yes, I can see how that's important."

"When I came back the house was locked."

"I'm sorry you didn't have anyone to help you through that. Does your grandmother live nearby?"

"No."

"Where does she live?"

"Oregon."

He made a note in my file. "I hear that you went to see your brother last night. What was that like?"

"I don't know. Weird, I guess."

"How did you like the Garlands?"

I shrugged.

"They liked you. They thought you were an articulate, intelligent girl and they really wanted you to stay and feel safe there. What made you decide to leave?"

I shrugged.

"That's okay. You don't need to tell me. But I do need your honest answer here: would it be okay if you stayed with the Garlands for a while?"

"Nothing's okay."

"Hmm. I suppose not. But we need a few days to straighten things out..."

Straighten things out. I laughed.

"...and I'd like to keep you and your brother together. Do you think you could stay with the Garlands for a bit? It would mean a lot to Prince."

I nodded.

"Good. I'm going to take you over there now. You can take a hot shower, get something to eat. You don't need to worry about your classes today. You have enough on your plate."

# NIGHT TWENTY THREE

The streetlights flickered like photonic butterflies trapped in glass and iron cages. There was an emptiness to the night, a tangible fragility I tiptoed on as I drifted through the vacant streets. My eyes no longer searched. They just swept along the pavement glazed over, focusing only inward. My feet glided forward automatically without coming all the way down to the ground. The half-empty fifth of whisky swung up and down like a pendulum. I was my own clock, marking the irregular seconds of my personal continuum of time and space.

Out here in the quiet of night, it was easy to imagine that some terrible plague had rolled through the neighborhood. I might have been the only person left. Even the few cars that rolled by occasionally were empty, driven by the ghosts in their own mechanical bodies.

I'd stayed with the Garlands all afternoon, through dinner, and until the whole house settled down to sleep. Then I crawled out of the tightly-tucked-in sheets, grabbed the first bottle of booze I could find, and snuck out the front door with no real destination in mind. I just needed to think.

When I reached the aqua house neatly trimmed in white, I stopped. Once upon a time I knew this house. I ran through its sprinklers and hung upside-down from that cherry tree when I was five and he was eight. He let me win each time we played Hide-and-seek but never when we ventured indoors for checkers or backgammon. But I broke the fairytale when I went out on that first date and let him shove his tongue all the way inside my mouth and his hands all the way up my shirt.

I didn't heed the warning that bubbled up from my stomach. Instead, I climbed the ladder, skipping over the broken rung, and came face to face with Tommy Nealer once more.

I froze, half in, half out.

"Artemis? What are you doing here?"

"I just need someplace quiet to think. I didn't know you still used this for anything."

"Just this," he said, holding up a joint.

He took another hit and reached his hand out to me, the ember facing toward him. I took it. I sucked in as much smoke as I could hold, letting it burn tiny black holes into my lungs just as my health teacher had warned. It hit me fast.

My head was already swimming, but I accepted the joint a second time anyway. We passed it back and forth, breathing deeply, sinking further and further underwater. We passed it until it diminished into a speck of rolled up paper that I could hardly hold onto. I put my mouth to it anyway, lapping up the last drops of smoke and twisting them around on my tongue.

Dazed, I floated up a few feet above myself and let everything melt away. Tommy was easy, like slipping back into a pair of old shoes that your parents harp on you to throw out but you can't because you know that nothing you buy in the store will fit this right.

We didn't speak at all. There was nothing to say.

My mind stumbled. My fingers moved in restless circles around my knees. My eyes refused to focus. They kept slipping between Tommy's hands and the seam of light and shadow that meet along the edge of his nose.

The image of Tommy expanded and filled my field of vision. He had moved closer to me, leaning forward in slow-mo, making me giggle uncontrollably. He got so close his nose crashed into mine.

And then his lips.

I pressed myself into him greedily, unexpectedly, just like old times.

But it wasn't the same. There was no heat, no fire. It was like kissing a machine. Disappointment dragged its claws across my chest. These weren't anything like the soft patient kisses Jason gave me in the volcano. Tommy's wet mouth tumbled into mine too fast, mixing the two of us together so thoroughly that we would not be able to separate cleanly at the end.

I swallowed the guilt that stabbed at my heart and let him kiss me more anyway. He slid his hands underneath my shirt and pants, unbuttoning and unzipping and unfastening. It happened so fast. Just like that we'd wiggled out of our clothes and were kissing harder, bodies smashed together.

I was drunk and high and lonely and desperate and Tommy was there. That's why I let it start.

But as soon as it did, I caught myself; I put my hands on Tommy's shoulders and said softly, "Stop."

And that was that.

He didn't fight me or tell me to come on like he did when we were dating. He just stopped.

"What's wrong?"

"I don't want this."

"Oh. Okay. I'm sorry. I thought you did. I'm sorry."

He helped me find my clothes.

"I thought you wanted to. I'm sorry."

"It's okay. I'm just not in a great place right now."

"I didn't hurt you, did I?"

"No. I'm okay."

"I'm sorry. I care about you a lot, you know. You're an amazing girl."

"I'm really not."

Clothed again, he lit up another joint, took a hit, and passed it to me, but I shook my head.

"I've been a jerk to you lately. I hope I'm not the reason that you're not feeling great."

I shook my head again.

"I still think about when we were together. I still miss you sometimes. I'm sorry if I hurt you."

I squirmed.

"It's just—I always felt like I could be myself around you. You're a lot of fun; I hope you know that. And you're going to do something really cool with yourself. I know it. I'm really sorry I've been such a douche lately."

"I should go."

"I'm sorry."

I smiled at him and shook his hand.

"Goodbye, Tommy."

He laughed, a little surprised. "Goodbye, Artemis. See you around."

I filled my eyes with him one last time and climbed out of the tree house to sneak back into bed next to Prince.

# DAY TWENTY FOUR

As soon as I got to school, they ushered me back into the principal's office once more. Rick was waiting for me. He asked me how I was and how I slept and if I ate and if I cried, and I told him everything that he expected to hear.

"We've been trying to get in touch with your grandmother," he said, "but she hasn't been answering the phone."

"She's in Singapore."

"Do you know when she's coming home?"

"No. Why?"

Rick took in a long breath. He sucked up so much air that there wasn't any left for me. "I'm going to tell you everything straight. I'm afraid you won't be returning to your mother's care. I'm sorry, I really am, but she relinquished custody of both you and your brother. It seems that she just doesn't want to get her life in order. I wish I had something better to report, but the paperwork just went through."

I stood and walked a few paces to the side, where I could watch myself. I looked pale, like someone had cut a hole in me and drained out all the blood.

"Did she say why?"

He took another long breath then let it go. "The reason stated was hardship."

I tried to stand—the other me, I mean, the one that asked the question, the one that I was watching—but my legs were soft like pudding and couldn't hold me up. The other me hit her knee on the way down. I cringed from across the room, but couldn't feel the pain, not from all the way over here.

"You'll be staying with the Garlands until we can get you and Prince permanently settled. We're hoping that your grandmother will agree to take you in. Your mother said she might."

"Can I have a minute?"

Rick looked around the room—maybe for sharp objects, I'm not sure. "Of course," he said at last and then drifted away.

*What do I do now?*

I floated closer to myself, but there was this tightness in my chest that made me feel like my heart was going to explode, so I had to back up again.

The other me gripped onto the sides of the chair with iron fists, staring straight ahead blindly. Rick had left his briefcase on the floor next to his chair. I had to jump up and down in front of it, practically waving my arms off before the other me saw it. Finally, she swiped my file and snuck into the teacher workroom through the back door. Together, we loaded it into the copier.

Mr. Bowman, my art teacher, was in there preparing for his next class.

"I thought students weren't supposed to use the copier."

"We're not."

"What are you copying?"

"The story of my life as told by Child Protective Services."

"Ohh," he winced. "I hear they do a terrible translation. Not at all like the real thing."

"There may be something useful in it."

"Such as?"

"Data."

"Ah."

I forced a smile and the machine put a staple through the papers for me.

"Alright, Miss Artemis. I'll leave you to your secrets."

By the time Rick returned, I'd tucked the original file back in his briefcase.

"When it rains it pours," was all he thought to say.

# NIGHT TWENTY FOUR

I ENTERED THROUGH THE SIDE door just before the band break. The gangly mix of forty-somethings disguised as teens played "What I Like About You," and the grown-ups danced. It looked just like our parties, only cast with heavier actors. They were freer than we were, unashamed by their large drunken movements. One man jumped onto each downbeat, smile wide, thinning hair flopping up and down with the music. A couple twirled a hole through the middle of the mob. They knew how to dance and the crowd gave them space to do it in. He spun her out a ways and brought her back in close. Too close. He held her body tight against his to prove that he loved her as much now as on the day they first danced this way.

I couldn't help it. I paused to smile at them.

Then, I searched the turbulent dance floor for evidence of my mother. I'd waited until the Garlands were sound asleep before I crept out the bedroom window. I had to find her. She was sure to turn up at one of these dives, and, if she could just see me, see that I came back, she'd change her mind. She'd have to. When the song ended, the band headed behind the scenes and the dancers out to smoke. That's when I saw him.

He hadn't been dancing. He sat at a small round table against the wall conspiring with a dizzy girl in a red dress. She looked young, too young, and the make-up around her eyes gobbed at the corners.

For a moment, I stood transfixed. My feet refused to move, holding onto the ground like two lead weights.

He turned his eyes to me, an instinct only. Meeting my gaze and rising a little, splashing his drink a bit on his shirt in the process, he made a motion as if to come toward me. I wanted to run but my legs had not yet returned to flesh.

A noisy crowd of bikers stepped between us, breaking the spell and granting me mobility. I slid over to him, in direct violation of the instinct that assured me it was better to flee. My legs led me around the crowd to the side; I didn't approach directly. I was a tiger stalking. I could even feel the heat of every black and orange stripe dripping down my skin.

I stood behind her, only a couple feet from him now. He still watched for me in the place I used to be, his face drained of its usual ruddiness as if I might have been a ghost.

I might have been.

When he turned and saw me standing there, he jumped, knocking into the table and sloshing the red-dress-girl's topply drink. He didn't seem to know whether to sit or stand and so did both alternately until he finally settled on neither.

"Artemis," was all he said.

I watched his mouth open and close like a fish gasping on the shore, losing to the air.

"You can't be in here," he finally continued. "How did you get in?"

"Through the door," I told him simply, squinting in the half-light.

"Go home."

"We don't have one anymore."

"Is this your kid?" the girl interrupted, speaking from her nose and sucking a piece of gum into her mouth. "She's cute."

I very nearly punched her in her poorly made-up face. I had never very nearly punched anyone before. Instead, I squeezed my hands into such tight balls that my nails drew blood.

"Is this the cell phone girl?" I asked.

"The cell phone girl?" they both asked.

"The one from the garbage disposal. From day one of the end of everything."

"Oh," my father said, finally sitting all the way down. "I'd forgotten. Yes."

"You forgot?" I repeated, the words making no sense when they spat out from my lips.

"What are you talking about?" said the cell phone girl.

"Yes, I forgot," he insisted. "I was a little drunk at the time."

"Do you want me to take her home?"

My eyes burned into his. "How could you forget something so important?"

"Do you want me to take you home, sweetie?"

"One night wasn't much different than any other. Sit down, Cherry."

"I'm just trying to help."

"That night was different. That was the night you ruined everything. You took everything that was good and balled it up and threw it in the trash. You took any chance I had at being a normal teenager away the day you left us."

He scoffed.

"It's true," I protested, but he didn't allow it.

"No. You were never going to be a normal teenager. Your mother saw to that." He took a sip of his drink. "I hadn't lived in that house in years, you know. What's the difference whether I'm there but not or not there at all?"

Cherry slapped at his hand as effectively as a kitten and just as fumbly with her movements. "Don't put your hand up to shoosh me."

"We needed you there to keep the world from falling to pieces," I said.

"It fell apart before you were even born."

"I'm your girlfriend, you know, not your slave."

I wanted to climb on the table and scream it into his ears so he would be able to hear. "It wasn't this bad. It was never this bad. It was never eviction notice or foster home bad before. You ruined everything."

"You're not the boss of me," the sloshy girl continued, too inebriated to care that no one heard her.

"Things are only as bad as you make them out to be. Why don't you consider this as an opportunity to start again," he waved his hands out as if to gather up the world for me, bellowing grandly. "You can live your own life, do the things you want to do—Cherry, baby, get out of my face—"

"What makes you think you have the right to talk to me like that?"

"You can enter the future without me there to fuck things up for you. Really," he concluded, bringing his glass to his lips again. "You're better off on you own. We all have to make that leap sometime. Why not now? Look, Cherry, why don't you go get us another round of drinks."

"Is your ex-wife here? Is that why this kid's knockin' around the bar?"

"You're walking out of my life? Just like that?"

He stood, and, seeing him rise, his floozy reached long nails out to tug at his pockets. "Get me another Appletini, would you?"

"I already did that. Now, I'm walking over to the bar."

"And tell the guy not to put so much Pucker in it this time. I don't like them so sour."

"Go home, Artemis."

"I don't have one."

He paused.

Cherry protested, "I thought you were getting us some more to drink."

"Then go back to whatever rat hole your mother crawled into and go to sleep and forget about me. Will you give me a minute to finish this conversation, Cherry? Jesus Christ."

"I'm thirsty."

I shouted, "She's gone. She's—"

"That's not my problem."

"I changed my mind. Make it a Cosmo."

"You want to come up with me? That way, you can tell him how to make it the way you like it?"

"I'm your daughter."

"That's debatable."

"Yeah, just let me get my purse."

"I have my own life to get back to. Go do something spectacular with yours—" He had already turned his face away.

With her ass in the air, Cherry dug beneath her chair. "It's down here somewhere."

"—and make enough money that you can afford a top notch therapist to unload all your problems on. Because, and really now—Seriously, Cherry, you're falling all over me, will you watch where you're stepping with those heels?"

"Sorry, they're just so wobbly from up here."

"You don't need me around fucking things up for you. I'm not worth it."

"I think I dropped my phone."

My father pulled one of the bouncers over. Pointing at me, he said, "This is a child. She doesn't belong in a bar."

They moved off to the counter where the irresponsible bartender poured them another round. I let the bouncer pull me away, and stood outside in the cold rain that wasn't there.

# DAY TWENTY FIVE

I WOKE UP ALONE IN Prince's bed. By the time I crept downstairs, he was already dressed and ready to go.

A clump of his hair was sticking out at a ridiculous angle but he wouldn't let me fix it. "Stop it," he complained, batting my hand away from his face. "You're going to make me be late."

I swung to the side when he pushed on my leg, as insubstantial as a paper doll.

"Have a good day at school," I said, but he was already tromping out the door. Charlotte met him there, smoothing the strand of unruly blonde hair back into place. He smiled when she touched his face. When he raised his hand to me, it was more of a dismissal than a wave.

Charlotte caught my eye. "Do you want a ride to school?"

"I'm not going."

"Why not?"

"What's the point?"

She shook her head and looked away.

"Okay. Are you going to be here when I get back?"

"I dunno. I might take a walk."

"Well, the spare keys are in the bowl. Lock up if you leave, okay?"

"Yeah."

She turned to Prince. "What are you looking forward to most at school today?"

He grinned up at her. "Today is library day. I'm going to borrow this many books and then read them all tonight." He showed her with his hands as many books as he could fit between them.

"Wow! That's a lot of books!"

"Not for me."

Though Charlotte closed the door softly, it made the empty house shake.

# NIGHT TWENTY FIVE

A DARK PURPLE SLIME OOZED up from the cracks in the ground and travelled through town, killing everything that it came across. So much poured out from under the skin of the Earth that it gathered into pools and streams until it became a wide river. I saw signs of its devastation everywhere. Bodies lay where they fell, staring up into the sky with glass eyes. Waterfront homes sat abandoned. No children played in these streets, not anymore. I walked through the ghost town until I came to the banks of the purple river and then I turned downstream and followed it along a decomposing boardwalk.

The planks rose above the slime high enough that the river could not bubble up through the cracks at my feet, but not nearly high enough for me to feel safely out of its way. I walked along in spite of the fear, avoiding the most deteriorated of the planks and wincing each time the platform creaked and sagged with my weight. The thought of this river feeding into an endless ocean of deadly goo made me shiver.

Nowhere else to go, I travelled downstream until the river swelled out wider and lapped up higher along the sides of the wood, splashing precariously close to my sprinting shoes.

A piece of the walkway had broken off and there was a five-foot gap in front of me. I skidded to a stop. On cue, a reminder of the destructive capabilities of the slime floated by face down. His arms were raised in eternal surrender.

Were I jumping across a creek, I wouldn't have thought twice. I could easily clear my own height: back up a bit, get a running start, and sail across with plenty of distance to spare. But if I missed at a creek, all I would be was wet. The two sides sat just far enough apart to make me doubt whether I could make the jump.

But there was nowhere else to go. I sucked in a trembling mouthful of air, fought the pounding pulse that shook each muscle, and leaped. I cleared the distance easily, but it was another half mile before the panicked tears dried up.

I saw the man in the balloon before he saw me. He stood in the basket, scratching his head, pondering his lack of flight.

"Hello," I said, coming to a stop.

He was too busy to respond.

"Hello? Do you need some help?"

"Hmm? Oh, yes. My balloon won't take off. I can't seem to force enough hot air in it to get this basket off the ground."

"Where are you trying to go?"

"Where to go? Where not to go? So many worlds out there, different than ours. This is no place to live anymore. Look around. This has become a place only to die."

"Isn't the purple slime everywhere? How will you get away?"

His eyes sparkled down to me and he leaned in close, revealing a secret. "There are plenty of other worlds, Diana of the Moon. Just because this is all we see and hear and smell does not make it all that Is. You yourself have travelled from another world to get here. One just needs to persist in the search for the doorways. They are all around."

"I don't remember another world."

"Ah. So easy to forget in the crossing. Doesn't mean you weren't somewhere else. Tell me, do you remember the moment of your birth?"

"No."

He raised his hands to the sky. "Who here does? Doesn't mean that it didn't happen. You've forgotten more than you remember. Try asking... What's his name?"

"Jason?"

"Yes, Jason. Try asking him to tell you the story of that trip the two of you took together. See how different he tells it. Might be surprised by how little you remember, and that was just a week ago. How much of your life has been utterly forgotten? And, if you can't even remember your own life, how could you hope to remember other lives in other worlds?"

I had my hands clasped on the edge of the basket.

"Well?" he asked, his eyes fixed firmly on mine.

"Well?"

"Are you going to help me lighten this balloon or not?"

"Oh."

I peered over the side to where he stood. I thought he was very tall, the way he towered above me. Now I could see that he was not, it was just that he was standing on a huge mound of three by five photos.

"Here's your problem," I told him. "Your basket is full of pictures."

He slapped himself on the forehead. "Of course! Photographs! Why didn't I think of that? Here, get rid of them."

"You don't want to keep them?"

"No, no! They're weighing me down. Toss them out, toss them out."

I reached into the basket and scooped out all the birthday parties and road trips and newborn relatives that kept him glued to the ground. I threw handful after handful into the river. They glittered as they slipped away below the light and succumbed to darkness. As I tossed the pictures away, the man shrunk shorter and shorter and the balloon strained higher and higher on its leads. Finally, I had thrown enough old memories into the river that the basket began to lift up. The man was still throwing his pictures out over the sides. They rained down on me.

"Wait!" I shouted to him. "Take me with you!"

He rose quickly now, fading into the distance. "Sorry, can't. I'm too high and besides, you have more work to do here. Good luck, Diana of the Moon!"

I watched him fly away until he was just a small red speck in the endless blue sky.

# DAY TWENTY SIX

Like a good secret agent, I had memorized my objectives and destroyed the evidence of my assignment. I arrived unarmed and alone, my motorcycle parked around the corner.

I was sweating so much I couldn't keep the palms of my hands dry. I just kept wiping them and wiping them against my pants but it didn't do any good. What if this didn't work? What if her heart didn't melt when she saw me? I should have brought Prince. No one could look at him and not soften like ice cream in the sun. Shit. My feet clanged up the metal steps and my heart knocked on the door for me.

When she answered in her pajamas, hair a mess, frowning, I backed away as if she were some animal that could bite me. I thought about running, turning around and getting the hell out of there and pretending that this never happened, that I didn't know where to find her. Maybe then some TV show could have reunited us in twenty years, once the wounds had scarred over and all that was left was a false memory of a happy childhood interrupted. But I didn't run.

My mother came outside and sat down next to me, lighting a cigarette. She offered me one, but I shook my head no.

"How did you find me?"

"The social worker."

"They supposed to give out my address?"

"No. I stole my file."

"Sounds about right."

A man came to the door, looked out at us and then retreated to the confines of the trailer.

"Who's that?"

"My boyfriend, Ted. He's a nice guy. He doesn't like kids."

"Oh." I'd never seen him before. I'd always pictured her wandering from bar to bar alone.

She smiled sadly and breathed through her cigarette.

"You don't want us anymore." It was a summary of the situation, not a question.

"No. It just wasn't working."

"So you're getting a divorce and instead of fighting about who gets to keep the kids you're fighting about who has to."

"No," she told me simply. "I wasn't cut out for all this motherhood shit. And, frankly, I was lousy at it. I can't be a mom. I'm 'unfit' and I sure as shit don't want to go to school to prove to the state or the feds or whatever that I can change. I ain't gonna change."

"What about Dad?"

"Your father denies that you're even his. You'll have a fight ahead if you wanna prove you are. But why bother? Fuck him, right. Piece of shit."

"Are we?"

"Hmm?"

"Are we his?"

"Probably. But what difference does it make? He doesn't want any part of any of it. Never did. Let him go, Miss. He ain't any good anyway."

"Your parents are supposed to fight for you."

"No one ever fought for me."

"What about Grandma? She would fight for you. She wouldn't give up like this. Leave us. She wouldn't do that."

"Bullshit."

"It's not."

"She did it all the time. Left us. Me and my sisters. We were alone for three weeks once. You don't know what it was like. You didn't know her then. You don't get to have a TV life. No one does. It's shit for everyone."

I looked away; watched a ladybug crawl all over the metal rail, lost.

"It's not fair."

"If you choose to feel that way."

"I didn't choose this. I didn't choose any of this."

"Well, neither did I."

"You did too choose this. You chose to have a child. You chose to have me."

"Not as much as you think. Sometimes life just throws shit at you and you don't dodge in time 'cause you don't know any better."

I wanted to cry but I didn't have any tears left. I sniffled into my sleeve but my eyes stayed dry. "Did you ever love us?"

"I still do. I just can't do this anymore."

"We can make it work. We weren't the best family but we made it work. We just need to try harder."

"It's over, Artemis. There's nothing left."

But I couldn't hear her anymore. "We can just go back to how it was. You'll see. It'll be fine. I'll take care of Prince and cook us dinner and keep the house in order, and you can sit with us while we watch cartoons in the morning, and Dad can get his job back, and we can be a family again. You loved him once; you can love him again. You just have to try harder."

"I never loved him."

"You're just not trying hard enough."

"No. I never loved him. Not really. I mean, I did the way you love a movie star, from a distance. He was handsome and rugged and much older and my parents hated him. I was young and stupid and I didn't know any better, so I ran away with him. If I was in love, it was only with the idea of him. But people aren't ideas. They're flesh and blood and lies and there comes a time when you have to see them for what they are and not what you hoped they were."

I shook my head.

"And you need to do that, too. We're not a family. We never were. We were just a bunch of strangers trying to hide out in the same house. I know you got some big dreams, kiddo. You gotta be free to chase them down. You're strong enough and you sure as shit got the brains. So go be something amazing, and when I call you to ask for money, you be too proud of yourself to give me any."

"You can't walk away from this. You can't just leave me."

"Well, according to the State of California I can."

She went back inside and shut the door.

# NIGHT TWENTY SIX

FARTHER DOWN THE BOARDWALK, I reached a young woman in a green dress. She stood on a stone wall gazing out across the purple river. If it weren't for the way her dress billowed leisurely in the wind, I might have thought she was a statue.

She sighed as I approached, never tearing her eyes away from the distant shore.

"Hi," I said.

She frowned and sunk down to sit on the edge of the wall, brown shoes tapping against the stones to the rhythm of a song I did not know.

"What's the matter?"

"We used to be one world," she answered without looking at me. "We crossed from here to there and back again without a thought."

She stopped, stood again, and squinted into the distance. Unsatisfied, she sat back down.

"Our world was pulled apart right before our eyes, but it happened so slowly that we didn't realize it until it was too late. We never thought to try to change the course of things; we didn't know that what was done could never be undone. One day, we simply woke up on one side or the other and that was that.

"I remember jumping from bank to bank when I was just a little girl. We dared each other to do it one-legged, or blindfolded, or backwards, knowing how dangerous the slime was. We should have held our lives in our hands cupped carefully like blown eggs. But we were so reckless with them in our youth. It made us feel alive. The slime could kill you; we knew that, everyone knew that. One drop was all it took. But it was a part of our lives. We grew up with it and we transformed it into a plaything.

"One morning, Micah jumped across and missed. We stayed away after that but not forever. The grown-ups built bridges so we could cross safely. First: small wooden ones. Then they made them out of iron and steel. But the river took them all. It grew wider each year until there was no longer any way across.

"Now, even the memory of the other side is distorted through the kaleidoscope of time so that what happened and what I only imagined are indistinguishable. The other side has become the memory of a childhood dream."

I stood next to her, looking with her, seeing nothing.

"Why do you still look across?" I asked.

"Because of what I've lost. We were maybe your age the last time I saw him—children, but grown-ups, too; in-betweeners who couldn't put their finger on which world we wanted most to inhabit. We played tag and Hide-and-seek and kissing games we pretended we invented.

"For a time, we could still stand on each shore and shout across. But it got harder and harder to hear him over the years. Now I can barely see him; he's just a speck in the distance."

"If you could, would you cross over to his side?"

"Of course."

"What if it meant that you could never come back here? That you would never see your family or your home again?"

She smiled, eyes still a mile away. "Whenever we leave we are gone for good. It is the nature of the journey."

I understood. I built her a boat and dragged it back to the boardwalk. She hadn't left her post.

"It won't work," she told me flatly. She had still never moved her eyes to mine.

"It will if I steer it."

"You can't know that for certain."

"Isn't it worth the risk?"

"To risk death to find love?" She turned to me now, her eyes burning like blue plasma: hot and dangerous. "I suppose it is."

We climbed onboard, dizzy with the danger. At least she had something to risk everything for. I had no excuse. I tossed my life to the whim of the river because I could; because I didn't have anything better to do with it. I was right, though, with the one oar in my hands the boat moved easily in a straight line toward the other shore, unaffected by the invisible current moving off to the sea.

Once across, she stepped out and reached her hand down to collect me.

But the river stole me away from the land. I tried to row and looked down to find that my paddle was only a burnt scar of wood. Helplessly, she stood on the edge of her future and watched me drift away.

Then the current picked up speed and I was gone.

# DAY TWENTY SEVEN

THERE WAS ONLY ONE WAY to put all the pieces back together and that was to capture Walker. I didn't know how I was going to do it but I knew where to find his burrow. I'd dig him out if I had to. I couldn't recover everything that Prince had lost but I could bring him back his bunny. He needed something to hold onto. It was the least I could do.

The streets between the Garlands' house and mine were quieter than I'd expected them to be. The whole world felt oddly abandoned.

I stopped in the empty driveway of my vacant house. It looked like all the others.

A scruffy-looking dog sat on the porch, his beady eyes following me. I'd never seen him before, but his tail thumped against the deck a few times as I approached, though he didn't get up to greet me. When I got within a few feet of him, he pulled his lips back into a toothy grin and let his tongue slide sideways out of his mouth.

"What's all over your face, dog?"

His fur was the color of rust, but it clumped funny around his mouth like it was sticky.

I reached down to pat him on the head and when I did, his tongue arched up between my fingers leaving a streak of saliva and blood on my palm.

Time stopped. I leapt over the railing, to the side of the house, and bolted into Prince's garden. The dog followed as if it were a game.

Walker lay on his side in the middle of the swirl of carrots. He'd dug some of them up early and the immature roots were scattered around him. With his back to me, he could have been asleep. But he didn't move when the dog pounced on him and he didn't struggle when it picked him up and tossed him into the sky. Blood leaked out through the hole in the front of him, splattering against my skin like cold rain.

"No!" I screamed and tackled the dog, my hands reaching into its mouth to take the broken body of Walker away, "No, no, no, no."

The dog wouldn't let go. It kept its teeth locked around my brother's bunny.

"No, no, no, no, no, no."

I forced both hands into its mouth, prying open its slippery jaws. Finally, its grip loosened and Walker fell to the ground. Then the dog's mouth closed on my hand.

I kicked it in the face as hard as I could, hugged the bloody shell of Walker against my body and fled to the house, bashing in one of the living room windows to gain entry. I slipped through the broken glass easily, but one of Walker's ears caught on the jagged window frame.

"No, no, no, no."

I freed him from the glass and laid him down on the kitchen counter.

He was hollow. The dog had left his skin intact but it had eaten most of him. I smoothed the back of his ears. They were still soft.

"I'm sorry."

I tried to pet him but it didn't work. I just kept smearing more blood all over him.

"I'm sorry. I'm sorry."

His body blurred. Tears poured out of my eyes.

"I'm sorry. I keep making everything worse."

My hand burned. I turned it over. The dog had ripped it open pretty bad and blood was pouring out of me at least as fast as tears.

"I have to clean this out," I said to Walker. "I'll be right back."

I drifted into the back bathroom to get a tube of Neosporin and returned with every bottle of pills in the house.

I lined them up in the pool of blood that had amassed in front of Walker.

Nine bottles.

I counted them again, just to be sure, and then I read the labels.

Vicodin, Advil, Aspirin, Hydrocodone, Ciprofloxacin, Hydrocortisone, Comtrex, Doxylamine, Alprazolam.

I didn't know what they were all for.

I slid them around so that they lined up from the biggest on the left to the smallest on the right. Then I remembered my hand and plucked the half-empty bottle of vodka off the coffee table. I put it against my lips and tipped it back until it pointed straight to the sky. When I came up for air, I poured a good deal of it onto my hand and let it burn.

I snapped off each lid, throwing them behind me. Most of the bottles only had a few pills left but I poured each one out and counted them anyway.

27, 3, 14, 2, 6, 1, 3, 4, 1.

Then I made the pills line up by size and counted them again.

3, 1, 2, 27, 14, 6, 1, 4, 3.

I kissed the bottle of vodka again, kissed Walker for the last time, and counted once more.

1, 2, 27, 14, 6, 1, 4, 3.

# NIGHT TWENTY SEVEN

Down I raced, faster and faster, caught in the current and unable to regain control. There was no way off this raggedy boat. The purple ooze splashed up along the sides and clung on with goopy fingers, burning away layer after layer of wood. It wouldn't take much longer for the river to digest the boat.

I scrunched myself into a ball, head down, eyes squeezed shut, as the river snapped and snarled and threw me about without mercy. On more than one occasion, the boat snagged on an eddy that whipped me around in a circle so fast I thought I was going to fly right out. I tried to regain control of my breathing, to force it to come and go in regular intervals, but it was no use. I could only suck up the air in tiny gasps and hiccough it out again unevenly.

For an hour or more, I travelled downstream like this: eyes closed, knees to my chest, arms hugged around me so tight they ached. I could only hope that when the boat was finally smashed to pieces, the river would swallow me in one gulp. A tiny voice inside me demanded that I raise my eyes and stare bravely on into the end. But I refused to listen. It couldn't make me.

Bam! The boat collided with something much larger and heavier than itself. I shrunk into a tinier ball, tighter toward myself. The river was flooding up along the sides of the broken vessel, I knew it. An inescapable rising tide. In a moment it would overcome the sides and rush toward me, filling all the empty space, erasing me from the world.

Eyes still closed, I waited for death.

But something in me wanted to see.

Something wanted to say goodbye to Prince and to Jason.

Something wanted to be a witness to the end of my days.

I lacked the courage.

I huddled closer against myself.

Nothing.

And still, nothing.

Trembling, I opened my eyes.

I had run aground against a pile of boulders in the center of the river. The boat was not broken. It bobbed casually in the still pool the rocks had formed, protected from the rushing current.

I climbed out and hoisted myself up to the top of the tallest stone, where I could see for miles all around. In the distance, a balloon drifted through the wide blue sky. It was him.

He was coming to take me home.

# DAY TWENTY EIGHT

I WOKE UP COVERED IN blood and vomit next to an empty vodka bottle. I don't think I drank it all. I think I dropped it and it spilled. I don't remember. I don't remember throwing up, either. I don't remember lying down and going to sleep. I don't remember how many pills I took.

I sat up to count them again. The room spun around me fast, and my head felt like it had split in two. Maybe the worst wasn't behind me yet.

A cold sweat leaked out across my skin. I wasn't ready to die. What had I done? I looked at the counter where the untaken pills sat in neat little rows. I hadn't made it very far down the line; most of the 27 Advil were still there. But I'd taken more than I should have. I knew that.

Standing, it turned out, wasn't an option, so I crawled out the front door, down the steps, and around the corner. I used my good hand to bang on the door.

Jason answered.

"Holy shit! Are you okay? What happened?"

"I don't want to die."

"Oh, my god."

He ran away. I must have looked like a monster, like a zombie crawling over to his house, rotten pieces falling off. I would have run from me, too.

"What happened to you? Is this your blood?" It was his mother.

"No, no, it's Walker's. He's dead."

"Are you hurt? Can you stand?"

"No. My head. My hand."

"Did you fall? Look at me in the eyes. Look at me."

I did as I was told. She was still wearing her scrubs. What time was it?

"Did you hit your head?"

"I don't know. I don't think so."

"But your head hurts when you stand?"

"Yes."

"Why?"

"I. I took some pills. And I drank some vodka. And the dog bit me. And I think I'm dying."

"When? When did you take the pills?"

"Yesterday. I don't know. Last night."

"Late last night?"

"No."

"What kind of pills did you take?"

"I don't remember. The six big ones and some of the Advil. Not all of them, just some of them."

"What were the big ones?"

"They were different. A couple were Comtrex. Some of them I think were antibiotics. But I don't know what kind."

"How many ibuprofen did you take?"

"What?"

"How many Advil? More than ten? More than twenty?"

"I don't know. Less than ten, I think. I can't remember. Am I going to die?"

"This is important. Did you take less than ten?"

"Yes. Yes. Less than ten. Am I going to die?"

"No, you're not going to die."

"What's wrong with me?"

"We're going to take you to the hospital. But you're going to be just fine."

Jason sat in the backseat with my head in his lap and smoothed out my filthy hair as his mom drove us to the doctor.

"I'm sorry."

"Shh. Tell me later."

"I never should have pushed you away. I'm so sorry. I miss you so much."

"Shh."

"They're gone."

"Who's gone?"

"My parents. They left us. Both of them. Prince has been in foster care. The house has been foreclosed. They're shipping us off to Oregon. I didn't know what to do."

"You could have come to me sooner."

"I didn't know how."

"I guess it doesn't matter now."

"I'm sorry."

"Don't."

"I love you, too."

"You're going to be okay," Jason's mother said.

We pulled into the hospital.

# NIGHT TWENTY EIGHT

At the hospital, I didn't tell them everything exactly as it happened. I told them about the dog and the vodka and about how much my hand hurt, and I told them that was why I took so many pills. Because of the pain.

I didn't lie. I just didn't tell them everything.

I didn't want to tell them about Walker. Or about how much it hurt inside. People understand outside pain. They understand dog bites and road rash and cuts from broken glass. But they just don't get the inside stuff. "Suck it up," they say. Or, "It's not as bad as you think it is." Or, "It'll feel better in the morning." And when you do something to make the inside pain go away, they blow it all out of proportion. I already knew it was a mistake. I didn't need everyone telling me something I already knew. So I didn't tell them the rest.

The doctors gave me fluids through an IV and the first of a series of rabies shots. They loaded me full of antibiotics and let me have a couple dozen Vicodin to take home.

Minus the vodka, it was just about the same concoction I'd taken the night before.

When they let Prince in, he crawled under the covers with me and kissed my bandaged hand about a hundred times.

"I missed you, Prince."

"But I'm right here."

"When I was gone. I missed you. You're the most important person in my life, you know that?"

He squeezed his arms around me. "You're my favorite sister."

"I'm your only sister."

"No. Out of all the sisters in the world you're my favorite. Out of all the thousands and hundreds and billions in the world."

I hugged him back, just as hard as I could. "And you're my favorite brother, out of all the thousands and hundreds and billions of brothers in the world. Don't ever forget that. I need you to know something. I need you to know that I'm always going to be there for you. That I'm never going to go away again. Okay?"

"Okay, Artemis."

"We're moving to Grandma's house. Did they tell you that?"

"Yes."

"You and me. We're going to live there together and things are going to be different, but that doesn't matter."

"Because we're going to stay together."

"That's right. Do you remember Grandma?"

"She smells like soap."

I laughed. "Prince?"

"Yeah?"

"I love you."

"I love you, too, silly sister."

# DAY TWENTY NINE

JASON'S MOTHER WAS RIGHT. I was going to be fine. Turns out all the vodka I drank helped me expel the pills out of my system. My mother's last gift. Never thought I'd be happy to throw up all over the living room. When I woke up at the Garlands' house the next day, I felt like none of it had happened.

Except for my hand. That hurt like a bitch.

In the afternoon, I appeared on Jason's doorstep with my helmet tucked under my arm and my bike parked out front.

"Not again," Jason pleaded, though through a smile. "I think I'll be missed this time."

"Not so far for this trip. Just a little ways up the mountain. I want to show you something."

"You're feeling better, then?"

"I still feel like I have a Walker-sized hole in my heart, but the hole in my head seems to have healed over."

Jason slipped out the front door, snuck around back to collect his helmet, and then ran down the block at full speed.

I hopped back on the bike and met him around the corner where he strapped on that ridiculous bright blue helmet and climbed on behind me. He hugged his arms around my waist just like before.

I drove east today, farther into the mountains, where I chose a side road that took us higher and higher, up away from the freeway. Jason kept me warm despite the cold wind that snapped at my skin with its alligator jaws.

I pulled over in front of a tree that I used to know and struck out along a trail that led into the forest. Jason ran along behind me. When the hill crested, we stopped to look down on the meadow below.

"I used to come here with my father when I was little, littler than Prince is now." I told him, letting my helmet fall to the ground. "He'd take me places, just the two of us, and invent adventures for us to go on. This was our favorite place. When we'd go into the meadow, it was just like we were entering another world. We built cities down there, whole kingdoms, and imagined we were on different planets, pioneers staking out a claim in a distant solar system. He made me feel important."

I sat on the hillside and watched the long-stemmed flowers sway in the breeze. I hadn't meant to talk at all. I thought I brought Jason out here to play in the field.

He sat next to me quietly, his shoulder touching mine.

"I know I shouldn't feel this way," I went on, "but I would give anything for things to be back the way they were. As shitty as that was, at least it was a known factor. I knew that when I got home from school my mother would be drunk on the couch and I would need to get dinner together for the three of us. I knew my father would return home late, just to sleep, and I knew that I could see him if I got up in the middle of the night and watched him from the doorway. I could count on sweeping up broken glass and skipping school to do the laundry."

Silently, Jason took my hand.

"But there were times when things were good. And even when it didn't seem that way, I could come out here and dig up one of my old treasure chests and hold the proof of it in my hands. I don't know how to move on."

"It's not easy to let go."

"I've been asked to surrender my identity. I'm no one's daughter. I'm without a home. I don't belong here. I don't belong anywhere. I don't know who I am anymore."

"You're the same person you always were. You aren't defined by these changes, Artemis. You experienced them and hopefully learned from them, but the essence of who you are doesn't waiver. You are a constant travelling through an unstable world."

I turned toward him. "I can't see it that way. I feel empty."

"That's because you don't know you the way I do."

"Who am I, Jason?"

"You're the dreamer," he whispered.

We walked hand in hand into the meadow and built a new city in the tall grasses. I wore a crown of poppies and left my name behind in a box of plastic horses.

# NIGHT TWENTY NINE

Later, leaning close to Jason and away from the cold of the late spring night, I whispered, "The planets used to call to me."

"Whole planets?"

I dismissed the joke in his tone and assured him, "Yes."

"What did they say?"

"They never said anything with words. They just glowed down at me and grew brighter and brighter and made me want to get up and run off as fast as I could. More than that. They made me need to run so fast there was no way to see where I was running to, or what I was running from."

"And now?"

"Now they seem still. They don't make me feel so restless." I slipped my fingers in between his. "They're quiet. I feel like I can stay put."

"And on the eve of your departure. How inconsiderate of them."

I laughed. "Do you get what I'm saying though?"

"Yes. I think I do."

"Do you feel that way sometimes?"

"Once," he began. "I dreamt that I was on a boat in the middle of the ocean. I had all these maps in front of me, along with a compass and a sextant, and I was trying to find my way to the New World. The problem was that I knew there was no New World left to be discovered. We had already filled in all the blank edges of the map and all the regions that used to warn 'Thar be dragons' were quiet islands and continents filled with nothing more frightening than people like ourselves. Even though in the dream I was on an old boat from the seventeenth century, I knew that there was nothing left for me to discover here.

"Then I saw Jupiter on the horizon. It was big, as big as the moon, and I wanted desperately to be able to sail over to it. I wanted to leave this world in favor of an undiscovered one."

"Did you make it?"

"No. I never reached the horizon. None of us ever do. It's just there to remind us to strive for something beyond ourselves."

We kissed beneath the galaxy.

# DAY THIRTY

It was late in the morning by the time I finally peeled open my eyes. I looked for Prince beside me, but, as I expected, he had already gone out. Paul and Charlotte had a garden, not a vegetable garden but one with flowers and ferns and soft leafy trees.

I found Charlotte in the kitchen.

"Do you like waffles?" she asked.

"Do you have a contingency plan if I say no?"

She laughed and shook her head. "No."

"I do. Like them, I mean." She was too sweet to jerk around.

I poured myself a cup of coffee with a generous portion of vanilla creamer.

Charlotte froze in place. "You drink coffee?"

"Of course I drink coffee. All kids drink coffee. This is a highly stimulated nation."

She laughed again, cracking eggs into a bowl.

"So, how did a couple of nice twenty-somethings like yourselves get into the business of fostering abandoned children?" I leaned against the counter and brought my coffee to my nose.

"We can't have a child of our own. The state makes it a lot easier to adopt if you register as a foster parent first."

I choked a little on my drink. I wasn't expecting such a straightforward answer. "How long have you been doing it?"

"There was a little boy, Caleb, that we had last month for a few days. Other than that, just you and Prince."

"How is it? Having two fucked up kids like me and Prince to deal with when what you really want is a baby of your own?"

"You're not fucked up."

My stomach tightened. "That word doesn't sound good on you."

"It doesn't sound good on you, either."

I frowned and lifted the mug up to my lips again. "We are, though, you know."

She stopped making waffles, right in the middle of step four, and turned her body toward mine. "What makes you think that?"

"Are you kidding? We've been disowned by both our parents, neither of which has been truly present in years. I kidnapped my best friend and ran off with him on a motorcycle. Right now, Prince is outside in your backyard philosophizing with a ladybug. We're not exactly normal."

Charlotte poured the batter into her waffle iron. "Nobody's normal. A girl as smart as you has no business believing in something so obviously imaginary."

My cheeks flushed.

"You'll be alright, Artemis. You'll make it through this. You've grown up too fast, is all." She released the waffle from its metal shell. "You still have time, though. You just need to take a step back and breathe again."

"Prince likes them with butter and syrup in each hole. And cut into tiny squares."

She smiled. "Maybe you should do it. I'll go get him."

I was careful only to cut along the center of each ridge.

☼ ☼ ☼

At sunset, I stood in front of the house with Jason. I wanted to halt the progression of time, to lock this instant away in a jar. That way I could look in on it every once in awhile and remember it for real.

"Will I see you again?" I asked him, fighting the tears that hung stubbornly to the corners of my eyes.

He laughed and wrapped his arms around me. "There is something here that's worth investigating, worth pursuing, worth falling in love with, and worth letting go of everything for. It goes without saying that there's something here worth waiting for. Our lives will cross again. What's a few years in the course of a lifetime?"

"What do we do now?"

"We go on with our lives. When the time comes for us to find each other again, the space will open up."

I pressed my face into his shoulder, leaving two wet circles in his shirt. "How do you know?"

"I know because it's what my heart tells me, just as obviously as my body tells me to hold you closer because you're so warm and just as obviously as my eyes tell me you are your most beautiful when you stand in the sunlight."

I pulled back from him just far enough to see my reflection in his eyes. "You gonna take a picture?"

"I don't need to. Good luck, Artemis. Live well."

I sunk into the backseat of the car and watched Jason watching me until he was only a tiny speck in the distance, and then, I closed my eyes and watched him closing his eyes, watching me.

# NIGHT THIRTY

I SAILED ACROSS A SMOOTH ocean under the soft glow of a half-full moon. The world was without noise, and, though I moved quickly across the water, everything was strangely still. In my bare feet, I walked to the bow, face to the wind. I held the guardrail for a moment in both my hands and I looked into the distance, past the ring of light around the boat, past the dark waves that stretched out in front of me.

There on the horizon, Mars was setting.

I took a breath in and climbed onto the rail, balancing on top of it and imagining that I was flying over the water on my own, that there was no boat to hold me up.

Below me, a pod of dolphins kept pace. They leaped into the crest of water at the nose of the boat and dipped again below the surface, disappearing into darkness. On a whim, I dove in with them.

Together we rolled along each wave, escorting the boat to safe harbor, somewhere far away, beyond where the sea holds the sky.

# DAY THIRTY ONE

When I opened the gate to let Prince into the garden, I knew not to expect a wonderland but he did not. I don't know whether he remembered this place or whether he only knew it from the hand-collected seeds our grandmother had sent him over the years, but he carried with him a vision of something bigger, greener, and more magical than what was really there. When Prince ran through the gate, he saw the old garden, the one from my dreams.

And then I saw it, too. The way it was supposed to be.

I rolled through the rows of vegetables and covered myself with a blanket of flowers to fool the butterflies into landing on my nose. I climbed the jacaranda and hung upside-down by my knees from one of its branches. I wrote Jason a poem on the back of a long strip of bark.

I remembered then what it was to be nine, and six, and two, and all the other ages I had hidden away from myself. I breathed for all these other Artemises, allowing them finally to run back into me, to come out of hiding and play in the sunlight.

# ACKNOWLEDGEMENTS

THREE YEARS AGO, I SET out on a journey with a spunky girl I didn't know. We could never have gotten this far without the countless people who helped us along the way. I did not write this book alone; it took a village.

Thank you, Mom, for always believing in me and teaching me to strive for the impossible. I don't know who I would have been if I couldn't have been a writer, and I couldn't have chosen so difficult a path if I didn't know that you had my back. Thank you for telling me that I could succeed and thank you for reading draft after draft and loving each one just because I wrote it.

Thank you, Connie, for always being ready to catch me when I fell and for giving to me freely, even when you weren't sure I was chasing a realistic dream. I could not have done this without your help.

Thank you Mom, James, Connie, Gaylen, Jamie, and Ed for letting me live in your houses while I worked on this book. I would write from a cardboard box if I needed to, so thank you for making sure I never did. And thank you also for putting up with me when the most I could say to you was, "Can't talk. Writing."

Thank you Tim, Kelley, Matt, and Jake, my early readers who believed in this project from the beginning.

Thank you to all the teachers who knew that I was a writer long before I did.

Thank you, Gene, for fostering a love of storytelling, Kathy for grading my creative essays with butterflies, and Ed for never giving me a grade at all.

Thank you to all my students who listened to my stories and asked me questions about them.

Thank you former seventh graders for being there at the moment of Artemis's birth and helping me bring her out into the world.

Thank you, April, for working tirelessly on my behalf.

Thank you, Leah, for coming back to Artemis again and again and for helping me transform that early draft into a real book.

Thank you, Cory, and the rest of the team at RainTown for making this dream a reality.

Thank you to everyone who finds themselves somewhere in these pages.

Thank you, Val, Lara, Gaylen, Mom, and many others for the stories you lived with me.

And, thank you, Ryan, for giving me a reason to write.

Photo by Tedshots

**Crystal Beran** has always wanted to fill in all the blank white spaces in the world with words. If she finished a math quiz early, she'd write a short story in the margins. If things were slow at work, the boss would find her scribbling away on paper coffee cups and the backs of customer receipts (she's had lots of jobs). If anyone tried to take away her paper, she'd just write on her hands and clothes. *Artemis Dreamt* is Crystal's first novel and she's already hard at work on her next book. Visit her at www.crystalberan.com, or at the beach, where she lives with her cat, Ariel, and python, Sam Clemens.

# MEET YOUR BOOKMAKERS

RAINTOWN PRESS
PORTLAND, OREGON

RAINTOWN PRESS IS PORTLAND, OREGON'S premier independent press dedicated to publishing classic and original literature for middle grade and young adult readers.

PORTLAND SERVES AS THE PERFECT backdrop for a press dedicated to young readers—the diversity of culture, literature and landscape here encourages us to be strong, autonomous, and even outright rebellious. There is a spirit of independent thinking and innovation paired with perseverance and tenacity among the people of the Northwest. Through the drudgery and gray skies, we not only survive, we thrive. We view the wet days we endure as being custom-made for reading a great book—or in our case, making one.

TO THAT END, WE SAY CLOSE THE UMBRELLA, AND...

## LET. IT. DRIZZLE.

RAINTOWN PRESS WOULD LIKE TO THANK: Leah Brown, for being the best editor, ever. We couldn't have *dreamt* up a better person for this job. To Mandi Russell, for your countless hours of hard work on this fantastic design. To Tara Lehmann, Rachel Moore, and Misty V'Marie for always hanging in there with us and helping out with pretty much everything else imagineable. And, although no longer with RainTown, the vitally important Anna Noak and Lucy Softich.